FAR FROM HOME

Georgia Blain published novels for adults and
young adults, essays, short stories, and a memoir.
Her first novel was the bestselling *Closed for Winter*,
which was made into a feature film. Her books have
been shortlisted for numerous awards including the
NSW, Victorian, and SA Premiers' Literary Awards,
the ALS Gold Medal, the Stella Prize, and the
Nita B. Kibble Award.

Georgia's works include *The Secret Lives of Men*,
Too Close to Home, the YA novels *Darkwater* and
Special, and *Between a Wolf and a Dog*, which was
shortlisted for the 2017 Stella Prize and awarded
the 2017 Victorian Premier's Literary Award for
Fiction and the 2016 University of Queensland
Fiction Book Award. Georgia passed away in
December 2016.

GEORGIA BLAIN

FAR FROM HOME

SCRIBE

Melbourne | London | Minneapolis

Scribe Publications
18–20 Edward St, Brunswick, Victoria 3056, Australia
2 John St, Clerkenwell, London, WC1N 2ES, United Kingdom
3754 Pleasant Ave, Suite 100, Minneapolis, Minnesota 55409, USA

First published by Scribe as *We All Lived in Bondi Then*
in Australia and New Zealand 2024
This edition published 2024

Typeset in Adobe Garamond Pro by the publishers.

Printed and bound in the UK by CPI Group (UK) Ltd,
Croydon CR0 4YY

Scribe is committed to the sustainable use of natural resources and
the use of paper products made responsibly from those resources.

978 1 957363 77 6 (paperback edition)
978 1 761385 71 1 (ebook)

scribepublications.com.au
scribepublications.co.uk
scribepublications.com

Foreword by Charlotte Wood i

Australia Square 1

Dear Professor Brewster 23

Far from home 57

Last days 75

Last one standing 91

Ship to shore 105

Still breathing 117

Sunday 135

We all lived in Bondi then 143

FOREWORD

BY CHARLOTTE WOOD

A short time after Georgia Blain died I discovered that I'd somehow deleted her voice messages from my phone. It was another devastating loss: I mourned those random, ordinary messages about nothing — about running late for coffee, how to cook burghul — because I couldn't bear never to hear her voice again.

Sometimes when I miss her now, I listen to our conversation about her work recorded for a writers' festival, or I find one of her many radio interviews still available online. I love to hear her speaking voice: clear, unsentimental, truthful, funny. Self-deprecating, yet completely unashamed.

Those same qualities are found in her writer's voice

— in her memoirs and essays and in her fiction, most especially her last, finest novel.

In 2016 Georgia's friend the writer James Bradley wrote that her memoir *Births Deaths Marriages* 'unlocked something in Georgia's work, liberating her somehow, for after it her writing shifted registers, becoming simultaneously more personal and more expansive'.

I agree with James. I think her work grew in stature and clarity, and in the expansive confidence he notes — the confidence to hide nothing of herself, even in the works most full of invention. Her last works shine with authority and truth and courage.

My grief for Georgia was also about the terrible unfairness of losing her work, just when her talent was approaching its height.

How precious then, to have these 'new' stories, written between 2012 and 2015. Georgia had read them again around the time she was finalising *Between a Wolf and a Dog*, intending to offer them as a collection at an appropriate interval after the novel's publication. Then life changed suddenly and other things, other work took priority, particularly the writings that became the magnificent, posthumously published *The Museum of Words: a memoir of language, writing, and mortality.*

But the stories remained, and now here they are.

These stories once again enter the terrain of Georgia's familiar preoccupations. She had, by the time she died, let go of any youthful shame about being drawn back and back to the same ground. In an interview in 2016 she told me:

> I [used to be] embarrassed about it — there was that male sort of notion that you had to write completely outside yourself, and you should be demonstrating a breadth of skill. But I'm not that kind of writer. And I'm not embarrassed anymore, because many writers I love — like Alice Munro and Richard Ford, for example — write into the same material over and over. And what you write in your twenties is very different from how you interpret things when you're fifty. You have quite a different angle on the same concerns.

It was Flaubert who said fiction is 'the response to a deep and always hidden wound'. But there was nothing hidden about the great wound in Georgia's family — the loss of her brother to schizophrenia and drug addiction at a young age — and over time she came to accept this loss as a natural wellspring for her fiction. This collection is no exception. But in these stories we also see exploration of another lifelong preoccupation — one hinted at beneath the fiction in *Between a Wolf and a Dog*, fully visible here: Georgia's deep and complicated attachment to her mother, and the new agony of watching her be consumed by Alzheimer's disease.

But of course, writing fiction 'close to home' is not the same as writing memoir. Like all good art, Georgia's fiction takes the intimate experience of her own life and *transforms* it, and in doing so reveals new and surprising discoveries for all of us.

Far from Home has an elegiac quality, often meditating on the isolating aftermath of loss: the parents in the devastating 'Ship to shore', unable to reach each other after the death of their child. The filmmaker sister in 'Australia Square', trying to reclaim her own sidelined experience of a terrible childhood incident while her brother still suffers the consequences. Or the regretful Annie in 'Last days', contemplating her lost self in motherhood.

The stories are complex, sometimes morphing from one 'subject' into quite another, like 'Dear Professor Brewster'. A daughter's account of her mother's slowly blossoming Alzheimer's disease is also an account of her father's absence — she being the child of an affair, her mother the eternal other woman — and of the almost-siblings she could have had, the mixed-up family with their mixed-up resentments and loyalties. It's a beautifully bevelled story; each time you turn it, it shows itself in a different light.

Youthful ambition's evaporation is another thread through these stories, often told from middle age, recalling the brutal clumsiness of youth. Twenty-something actors, writers, filmmakers, musicians, and dancers parade gorgeously through share-house parties in their op-shop finery, glittering with potential, drug-heightened recklessness, lust, and destined fame. As one narrator says: 'my hopes and desires and plans all unsullied, the self that I was to become beckoning, waiting'. These artists in waiting reappear decades later in accidental meetings, now ruefully teaching drama in high school or managing music-licensing databases, chastened by the years and reality's bruises. It's testament to Georgia's clear-eyed vision that these transformations contain no lessons, no authorial judgements — simply her compassionate observation of the ways life has of turning out differently than we'd hoped.

Okay, maybe there's the occasional judgement. Sometimes Georgia's dark wit can't resist a brief, delicious satirical impulse, as with aspiring novelist boyfriend Nate in 'Still breathing'.

> He worked as a waiter at night and had been writing a novel for years. At first I listened when he told me what it was about … The central character was in a coma, able to hear the thoughts of his family and friends who gathered around his bedside, but unable to utter a word himself.
>
> Nate wrote well, and I didn't mind listening. The problem was that he didn't know how to create an entire tale around his idea, and so it had stayed poised, stuck in the middle, sagging with the weight of each polish he gave in place of progress.

Naturally, when the young narrator is poleaxed by glandular fever, feverishly sweating and immobilised, Nate is unable to help. He stands outside her bedroom window, fearing contagion, and explains that he can't look after her because 'I've just gotta finish the book.'

I doubt I'll be the only writer cringing in recognition of the Nate in my younger self.

Then, there are the dogs. Old dogs, disobedient dogs, abandoned dogs, mysterious telephone-answering dogs, dogs named Dotty and Pixie and Edna plod and skitter their way through these pages. Dying dogs, who carry meaning and knowledge we humans overlook or ignore, but who lead us to things we need to see. 'You can't close their eyes when they die,' says a child in 'Last one standing', and the narrator finds that it's true.

Things are still to be seen, difficult things, following a death.

In 'Australia Square', the narrator discovers her late mother's obsessive notes and diaries, documenting attempts to make sense of the event that changed the family forever. The middle-aged narrator learns that she and her mother shared the same recurring dream of the calamity in one of these diaries.

> I'd held it with trepidation, hoping I would find a
> clear, concise explanation for her relentless attempts
> to retrieve my brother's memory, perhaps some aware-
> ness of her own madness, maybe it was an apology I

wanted, or a glimpse of softness and love, even regret that she had lost me.

They were all there.

And then I put the book away. It was just one slim volume amidst piles of notes and tapes, a few words that revealed another hidden, but not definitive, self.

I had found something secret, but that did not mean I had found her.

This ending shows us what Georgia always knew, what her writing has always told us: there are no easy answers. No clear conclusions will emerge to save us. Life will do with us what it will, and our only task is to love one another as best we can. Like the bereaved couple lying mute in the dark, Georgia's clear, insightful voice tells us this is our only duty: to keep sending those whispered signals out and back, ship to shore, shore to lost ship.

Charlotte Wood

AUSTRALIA SQUARE

When I was five years old, we had a nanny. Not that we called her that. She was Mathilde, and if we tried to explain who she was to outsiders, she was the housekeeper. She cooked our meals, cleaned, took care of us during the day, and put us to bed.

My mother and father both worked. My father was a stockbroker and my mother was a family therapist. Her rooms were at the bottom of a terrace house in Balmain. She had seagrass matting on the floor, a bed with an Indian bedspread, beanbags, and a coffee table from Morocco. At that stage, she specialised in group therapy, and was renowned for her success with teenagers.

My father's office was in the city, right near the top of Australia Square, a building that was then the tallest in the country and with a name that never made sense to me.

1

'But it's round,' I would say whenever we went there to meet him for lunch.

Mathilde took us.

She was only nineteen. She had come from France, wanting to learn English and travel the world. We had no spare bedroom so she shared with my brother, Lewis, who was just six months old.

Although I wouldn't have realised it at the time, Lewis was the mistake, the pregnancy that happened as my parents' marriage was coming to an end, a baby who had learnt to be quiet, well behaved, and undemanding in order not to put any further stress on the circumstances.

I loved him. I dressed him like a doll, and bathed him, and lifted him, my own small body straining with his weight as I lowered him into his pram, making sure he had his favourite blanket tucked around his legs and the square of muslin he liked to clutch and softly fan against his cheek as he sucked his thumb.

Mathilde also loved him, cooing to him in French as she fed him mashed-up banana or cottage cheese, carefully wiping his mouth with a damp cloth when he'd finished.

When she took us to visit my father, we had to catch a ferry and a bus into the city, a trip that took us close to an hour. On that particular day, Mathilde was taking us in to have lunch with my father because she needed to see a dentist.

'It is a terrible pain,' she said in her heavily accented

English, as she held her hand over her cheek and winced. 'Like hammers and drills, bzzzzz, right here.' She sat back on the ferry's hard wooden bench and closed her eyes to the warmth of the sun and salty spray of the harbour, while I played peekaboo with Lewis, now you see me, now you don't.

Mathilde knew the ferry hand at the Quay. He helped her lift the pram down the ramp, a cigarette in the corner of his mouth, his grin cheeky as he told her she was too young and beautiful to be tied down like this.

She rolled her eyes at him, before taking one of the cigarettes he offered, her long chestnut hair a smooth sheet as she leant forward so that he could light it for her. The pontoon rocked with the slapping of the tide, and I could smell diesel fumes. Seagulls squawked as they fought over the crust of a sandwich.

In the shade with Lewis, I watched as they talked, the deckhand wanting to find out which ferry we would be on in the afternoon, Mathilde pretending to understand less than she did.

'He smells too much. The oil,' she said, wrinkling her nose. 'And grease on his hands.' But still there was a slight smile on her face as she went through the barricades without looking back at him once.

We didn't catch the bus that day. Mathilde wanted to walk. She was getting fat, she complained to me, looking down at her slim tanned legs, long and shapely beneath a faded cotton miniskirt. 'It is no good if I am like the elephant. At home, they will say: "Mathilde, quel dommage!" They will think I had too many of the meat pies.' She walked briskly as she spoke, and I had difficulty keeping up, frequently having to break into a run or a skip as she veered the pram through the crowds on George Street.

'Now,' she said, and she knelt down close to me, smoothing my hair and kissing me on each cheek. 'I will take you and your beautiful brother up to the top and I will give you to your father. You will be good, non?' She straightened Lewis' blanket and tucked in the edges. He was asleep, waxy eyelids pinky blue, cheeks pale in the shade.

Mathilde checked her reflection in the window, tugging a little at the hem of her skirt and adjusting her blouse. She did not flirt openly with my father; it was a more a matter of ensuring that she stood at the right angle, that she leant that little bit closer, that her smile had that slightly secretive tilt, even when she had a toothache. She was young and beautiful and she enjoyed the effect she had on men, but she was also respectable. She knew the boundaries.

My father always behaved impeccably. He was kind to her and interested in her attempts at conversing with him, gently correcting her English, which was always a little poorer — more in need of assistance — when she was with him. And then he would disentangle himself with that smooth ease he had, moving back towards his desk and picking up his phone as he said farewell.

He worked on the forty-seventh floor, in an office that looked out over the pale haze of the city skyline, the sweep of new roads and construction, toy-like beneath him. Years later, when he told me how much his job bored him, he admitted to loving the distance of that view, the world small and quiet and calm, far away in its silence.

I had brought my toy pony with me that day. I took it most places, cupping it in the palm of my hand and letting it trot along a balcony edge or gallop along a seat or table, whispering stories to myself as I did so, tales of the close bond between myself and that horse. He was called Blaze, an unimaginative name, I know — also not particularly apt, as he was white, with no markings at all.

It was when the lift doors opened that I realised I did not have him. I panicked. I must have dropped him, and I looked to the ground before turning to run back to the entrance, perhaps even the street to find him. Mathilde stepped out to stop me, her hand reaching for mine. She left the lift for only a moment, but long enough for its doors to close, shutting on Lewis, who was inside, fast asleep in his pram.

And that was it.

Such a simple mistake.

An accident that could have happened to anyone.

We were there in the lobby, and Lewis was gone.

* * *

The documentary premiere was held in a small theatre. I hadn't expected Lewis to attend; after all, he had insisted on not being interviewed. But he was there, his bulk slouched in a grubby woollen seat near the back, legs sticking out into the aisle, clapping slowly and loudly as everyone filed out.

It was our father who dealt with him. He gently disengaged himself from an eager woman who was telling him how she remembered my mother as a fascinating but difficult creature — 'demanding,' she said, nodding energetically, as my father apologised for being so rude, but he needed to catch his son before he left.

His hand resting gently on Lewis' shoulder, he talked to him softly for a few moments, and then he sat with him, one arm around him.

I looked away, scared that I might cry. There were people waiting to congratulate me: friends, others who had worked on the film, people I knew well, and some I didn't know at all.

Brave, they said. *Honest*. Or else they wanted to talk about my mother — to speak of their own memories of her, or to proffer an opinion on her character and our childhood.

I thanked them, embarrassed, frequently glancing back to see if my father and Lewis were still there.

As the last people began to leave, a tall, slender woman approached. She had short greying hair, tanned skin, and an elegant shift dress, a thick silver cuff encircling her wrist. There was something familiar about her, the twist of her mouth as she looked at me, momentarily shy, hesitant, before wrapping her arms around me, the smell of bergamot and mandarin sharp and clean on her skin.

'It's me,' she said, the accent much less pronounced than it used to be, but still there, unmistakeable.

'Mathilde?'

'I did not know if you would want to see me, but, I — I need to, I needed to be here. It has not been since then, since that day.'

This was the first time she had come back to this country. Her words were tangled, tripping over each other, as she said she had wanted to call since she had arrived a week ago, but, 'I lost the nerve, you know?' She shook her head. 'And then I saw you had this film and it was like, how you say? Fate. It was good for me. Hard. But good for me.'

Her skin was lined, grooved by the sun, and she had a tic in one eye — small imperfections that I hadn't noticed when I first saw her.

'You have time for a drink?' she asked.

I told her my father was here. And Lewis. We were going out to dinner.

She took her hand off my arm, flinching slightly. 'Of course,' she said, 'of course,' and she glanced nervously behind her.

'Gerard will be fine,' I said, but I could not speak for Lewis. No one could speak for Lewis.

They were both still there at the back of the room, and I took her over, my hand clutching hers, just as it had when I was a child, but this time I was the one looking out for her.

'It's Mathilde,' I said to my father.

He glanced up, pale blue eyes fixed on her, the sheen of tears so faint as to have been imperceptible to those who did not know him as well as I did, before he stood, frail on his feet, and held his hand out to her.

He was about to greet her, to tell her how good it was to see her again, in fact, his mouth was open to speak and he would have uttered the words, were it not for Lewis, who laughed in that loud manner he had, a sound that was utterly disconnected from the distress on his face.

'You know what happened?' he said to Mathilde. 'I was taken by aliens,' and he nodded vehemently. 'Repeatedly.' He kept nodding. 'I gave birth to twenty-seven of their plastic children and they are descending to earth to take over. I knew you were coming.' He began to rock a little, as he always did when he didn't take medication and became stressed. 'They told me you were coming.' He pointed at her silver cuff. 'That is their microphone.'

She did not miss a beat.

'Ah, Lewis,' she said, and she took the seat next to him. 'I am so sorry. I am so sorry for it all.'

* * *

There are fifty floors in Australia Square, and we caught a lift to each one, Mathilde and I, pressing every button and begging the other passengers to hold the door, just for a moment, while we looked.

I believe we checked every lobby, but I don't really know. We became increasingly panicked as we ascended higher and higher.

'Lewis,' Mathilde called as she ran out. 'Lewis!' As though he were capable of responding to his name.

One of the receptionists tried to calm her, but Mathilde just brushed her aside. Another called security. 'Tell him he is only six months, in the pram,' Mathilde shouted as the lift door shut in front of us again.

We went right to the top, to the revolving restaurant that always made me feel car sick, the whole world below shifting without any apparent effort. They were serving the first lunches, the dining area hushed, the maître d' trying to calm Mathilde as he spoke to her in French.

And then we went down again, to my father, working in his office on the forty-seventh floor.

I can't remember many of the details of what followed. I know there was a search. First everyone in the office — each person taking a separate group of floors. Next the security guard, and then, of course, the police. My father's calm soothed us all, but as the brilliance of the noon sunshine slipped into early afternoon, as the police questioned us over and over again, and as my father told us it was time to call my mother, his calm began to fracture. I watched as he brushed his hair back from his face, and, hand shaking, lit the cigarette his secretary, Louise, had given him. He only ever smoked on Christmas Day, and just one cigar after breakfast.

I was sitting on the floor of his office. Mathilde had gone — I don't know where, perhaps to the dentist, perhaps to speak to the police again.

My father's hand trembled as he raised the cigarette to his mouth, drew back once, and then stubbed it out. He was steady again as he dialled my mother's number, waiting for her to pick up, but then when he spoke, he shattered. I had never seen him weep. I had never seen him display anything other than a kind distance. I sat there on the floor, knees hugged to my chest, as he told her that Lewis was missing, and I, too, began to cry, now fully aware that this was as serious as I had suspected.

Lewis laughed through most of the dinner with Mathilde. It had been a long time since I had seen him that psychotic. It was the film, I supposed, and perhaps seeing Mathilde again, although I don't know how he would have framed his recollections of her.

He hadn't seen her since he was six months old. The memories we form at that time are so difficult to access. But then, he was a man whose memory had been probed and pushed and slapped and coaxed and shouted at and whispered to, over and over again. He was a man who housed a memory that had obsessed my mother — it was a glittering, pulsating, glowing ember that she was reaching for, constantly, hand stretched out, only to have it recede each time she tried to grasp it. For most of us, there would be no recollection of someone we knew when we were so young, nothing other than just a sense of who they are through stories we might have heard, pictures we had been shown, and, perhaps, somewhere deep inside, a sense of that person's love or hatred or indifference in the way in which we have built our self, like a smear of mortar between the blocks.

We ate at a restaurant near the cinema, Lewis talking energetically to his roast chicken, leaning close and scolding it for being so rude about Mathilde, and then he would look across at her and wag his finger in her face.

'Tell them I'm not listening,' he said. 'I'm not their slave.'

When he became particularly agitated, my father soothed him by rubbing his hand on his arm, hushing him as though he were a baby again.

Needless to say, it was hard to talk. Mathilde tried valiantly to ask us questions, to tell us a little about her life — she lived in London now and was teaching French at a girl's school, she'd never had children — small facts thrown hopefully across the insanity that engulfed us whenever Lewis was like this.

'He needs to go back on medication,' I told my father as we left, Lewis pacing up and down the street, muttering to himself. 'I shouldn't have made the film,' I uttered by way of a feeble apology. The truth was I'd known that he would find it difficult to deal with and I'd gone ahead anyway, telling myself that I was an artist, this was my job, I couldn't have my life ruled by my brother's mental illness. I'd made my choice and to pretend that I was sorry now was pathetic. I hugged my father, more sorry for the stress that it put him under, knowing that if I voiced this he would tell me it was okay, he wanted me to live my life fully.

And then he looked at me, tired and old.

'Your mother loved you both,' he said.

I nodded.

'She was distraught.'

I squeezed his hand.

'I think I'll need to get him to hospital tomorrow,' he looked in the direction of Lewis. 'Poor boy. Poor boy.'

I knew he dreaded it. He was the only person capable of talking him into going. I had seen him, sitting calmly with Lewis for hours on end, finding a fine thread that cut through the madness, just enough to slowly bring him in, like roping a wild horse — calm and patience, calm and patience.

'I don't know what I'll do when Gerard dies,' I told Mathilde as I drove her home.

She looked at me in the darkness of the car, her dark brown eyes catching the dash light as she shook her head.

'He isn't always that bad,' I added, referring to Lewis

now. 'Tonight was the worst I have seen him in a long time.'

She stroked the side of my face as I pulled over outside her hotel. 'But you?' she asked. 'You are well? Your life? It is good?'

I smiled and told her what she wanted to hear, which wasn't so far from the truth. I had work I liked — although never quite enough. I had love, too — although never of the lasting kind.

She was here for a week, she said. If I had time to see her again, she would like that. She kissed me on the cheek and for an instant I felt like a child again, back in my bed, Mathilde leaning over me, whispering good night. 'Bon nuit, ma petite, bon nuit.' Through my window, I could see the darkness of the sky, freckled with stars, the evening breeze lifting the curtain. Downstairs, I could hear my parents' dinner party, laughter, the sound of a cork popping, glasses clinking — my mother liked entertaining — and if I glanced across the hall, there was a sliver of light under Lewis' door. Mathilde would be lying on her bed while he slept, reading probably, while beside her Lewis breathed easy.

It is hard to know what I remember. When I made my film, I pieced together a story from my own recollections and the recollections of others: my father, my parents' friends, my mother's colleagues, and those of her patients who were willing to talk. I had tried to contact Mathilde as well, but I had no luck. My mother had hired her, my father said. He knew very little about her details. As soon as the police cleared her, she returned to France, not wanting to stay in touch.

I was not trying to solve the mystery. I was just wanting to make sense of it all — and particularly of my mother, whose actions became progressively more incomprehensible to me the older I became.

At the end of the process, I'm not sure if I achieved anything more than an ordering, an arrangement of cards that could so easily be reshuffled and placed in a different sequence.

My recollection of those two weeks in which we did not know what had happened to Lewis are purely sensory. I was living in an electrically charged vault, each touch generating a shock, all of us red raw, flayed. At first my mother was ferocious, furious with Mathilde, shouting and screaming at her to leave, to get out (which she did), furious with the police for not doing their job, raging at the world, and at my father for not displaying the emotion she needed and wanted. At least this is what I think I remember. But some of her friends told me a different story, one describing her as catatonic in her despair, unable to eat, sleep, or talk to anyone.

My father returned to work, retreating into himself.

I was left alone, frequently looked after by a neighbour who was always on the phone speaking of the tragedy in hushed tones, eyes wide with the importance of it all.

Other than a sense of the shape of that time and an awareness of the charged particles around us all, I do have one strong visual memory, and it is of my mother.

I came home to find her seated at the bottom of the stairs in her bra and underpants, hair dishevelled, make-up smeared. At the time I would not have known she was drunk — there was simply something very wrong with seeing her like that. Normally an elegant woman who wore flared jeans and T-shirts with a style that most people never attained, and only a little mascara and a pale lipstick, she was energetic, alive, busy, focused in the moments when she turned her gaze on me. There on the stairs, though, she was bleary, wanton, despairing, her lack of clothes slapping a layer of sexuality onto her grief that disturbed me enough to cry out and rush to her, wanting her to comfort me.

But she couldn't.

Of course she couldn't.

And as I remember standing in front of her, I see a man there, at the top of the stairs.

Or is there?

Perhaps it is simply the sight of my mother in her underwear that leads me to place him in the scene, or perhaps it is the knowledge that she left my father soon after this moment, moving in with a man who was considerably younger than her and had several other girlfriends — a man I was instructed to call Ralph, and who was soon replaced by Marc and then Denise or Jenny, and then, finally, solitude, her obsession with Lewis leaving no room for anything else.

Two days after the film was shown, I met Mathilde for lunch. In the bright sunshine, she looked older, and when she took off her sunglasses to greet me, the tic in her eye was more pronounced than it had seemed two nights earlier.

She ordered a salad and a mineral water, wanting to move outside so she could smoke.

'You can't,' I told her. 'It's banned everywhere.'

She shook her head. 'So what are we meant to do? Us people who are addicted? And who are, how do you say it?' She smiled. 'Nervous without a cigarette?'

I also smiled. 'You could twist your napkin,' I suggested. 'Or chew your fingernails?'

She laughed. 'Never.' She held her hands out and they were beautifully manicured, long oval fingernails deftly coated with clear polish.

'I was young,' she told me then. 'Too young to be left alone with two children. But I do not think I was irresponsible.' She shook her head. 'It has troubled me, you know? What could I have done? I should have held onto the pram when I reached for you but I didn't, you know? And then, it wasn't alright. Sometimes you make these mistakes and it is okay. And just sometimes, when you do not know it, it is not okay. Not okay at all.'

* * *

Lewis was found a fortnight after he went missing.

He was left at a police station in his pram. His clothes had been changed. He was in a nappy and a pale blue singlet — his terry-towelling shorts and T-shirt gone. He still had his favourite blanket, but the square of muslin he clutched when he sucked his thumb was no longer with him. In the basket underneath was his bottle, clean and dry, and lying next to it, my white horse.

There was no note. No indication of where he had been or who had returned him.

The doctors examined his body, checking carefully for signs of harm or 'interference', as they called it.

It seemed there were none.

'Are you sure it's him?' I asked, or at least this is what my father told me when I interviewed him for the film.

'You didn't believe it. You checked him again and again.' He smiled. 'Sometimes I wondered myself. Maybe it wasn't him.' He shook his head.

'But there was the horse,' I reminded him, and the same pram, and his blanket.

'I know.' He looked sad then, but I held the camera on him, aware he was thinking what I was thinking. What had happened to the calm boy who used to live with us?

Because he cried, constantly. He screamed and yelled and howled, and as he grew older, he threw tantrums that would render everyone in their vicinity helpless to their force.

We lived with my mother then — and whoever was sharing her bed.

We had to let him express himself.

'There's trauma,' she told us. 'He needs to let it out.'

And then, when Lewis was old enough to talk, her serious work began.

My mother sent Mathilde an aerogramme, typed, the news of his discovery briskly dealt with, followed by a request that she return to Australia, that she may be helpful in trying to retrieve his memory of those two weeks.

'I was hurt,' Mathilde explained. 'She did not tell me until so long after he was found. And I did not want this. Not to come back to what happened. I did not understand what she thought I could do.'

Mathilde had barely eaten any of her salad. She lifted her sunglasses and looked at me. 'When I was nineteen, I was just a girl. I liked children. I liked you and your brother. I liked having fun. I thought I would meet a man who was rich and handsome and I would marry him and have babies of my own.' She smiled. 'Or perhaps I would be, how you say, discovered? I would be famous. In the movies. These ideas, they were the ideas of a silly girl.'

She signalled the waiter, asking if she could order a glass of hot water with a slice of lemon, and she turned back to me. 'Your mother, what she did was wrong.'

I knew that.

I suppose I always knew it, but it wasn't until I turned sixteen and we fought, a bitter, angry fight, in which I accused her of being obsessive, cruel, unloving, mad, flinging every foul moniker I could lay my hands on in her direction, a never-ending barrel of arsenal at my feet — it wasn't until then that I tried to break free.

When she died and my father and I cleared out her office, we didn't want to look at her recordings, notes, and articles, the overwhelming documentation of her quest to retrieve Lewis' memory, neatly catalogued and ordered. She'd begun with straight therapy sessions, talk, perhaps a little play-acting, before shifting to hypnotherapy, and finally, at the time I left, she'd turned to controlled sessions with him on various psychotropic drugs. Four years after her death, when I decided to make my film, I opened the boxes.

I started with the notes first, thinking they would be easier than the recordings. But watching Lewis ramble and rant on film, or listening to him on tape, was not as difficult as I had expected. It was reading my mother's words that frequently made me stop, the paper pushed to one side as I caught my breath. She was a fierce woman, sharp, unable to suffer a fool, quick to cut you down with statements that were honed, truthful, but frequently lacking in any delicacy or care. She summarised each of Lewis' responses with a clinical precision that denied any sense of him as a person, let alone her love for him as her son.

And then at the bottom of the box was her personal diary.

I opened it and a photograph fell out. She was young — in her late twenties, pale blonde hair falling across her face, clear eyes, big wide mouth open in a laugh as she held Lewis up in her arms, a beautiful round baby, giggling in delight.

'It was fear.' Mathilde shook her head. 'I think that is it. She did not know what had happened to him. Perhaps when you do not know you are more afraid.'

I found it hard to think of my mother as afraid.

In all the years in which I ran from her, throwing myself into increasing trouble, she never even flinched.

'Do you know she was a downhill skier?' I asked Mathilde.

She laughed. 'Here? In this country? With no mountains?'

Her father had been an engineer, I said. They lived in Switzerland until she was sixteen. There was talk of her competing internationally.

But she met Gerard and she fell in love with him. She was pregnant at nineteen, about to become a mother to me.

I asked Mathilde if she had gone back there: to that tower.

She looked at me. 'On the day I arrived. It was just a building.'

'I used to go every day.' I looked up at the sky as I spoke. 'After I ran away from her. I caught the lift to the top and then down again. I did it for a month.'

'And then you stopped?'

I nodded, although I still dream of it sometimes, the doors opening, but never quite wide enough to let me really see if it is him, and sometimes I am afraid, terribly afraid for him, while at other times I am at peace, because I know he is okay, he is in his pram and he is with someone who loves him.

My mother had the same dream. I know. It was in her diary.

I'd held it with trepidation, hoping I would find a clear, concise explanation for her relentless attempts to retrieve my brother's memory, perhaps some awareness of her own madness, maybe it was an apology I wanted, or a glimpse of softness and love, even regret that she had lost me.

They were all there.

And then I put the book away. It was just one slim volume amidst piles of notes and tapes, a few words that revealed another hidden, but not definitive, self.

I had found something secret, but that did not mean I had found her.

DEAR PROFESSOR BREWSTER

Dear Professor Brewster,

I am Alice Longmire's daughter and I am writing to you because I have become increasingly concerned about my mother's memory.

I realise she is your patient and your relationship is confidential, but I wanted you to know what's been happening, as she is unlikely to tell you herself.

She has always been vague and forgetful, but it is worsening. She calls me and then forgets she has rung an hour later; or she tells me the same story several times in an afternoon. I was particularly concerned by a recent episode in which she completely confused night and day. She got up when it was dark but was sure it was daytime, and wondered why everything was shut. She went to a friend's house for what she thought was breakfast, only to find her eating dinner and drinking wine, much to her confusion. When she relayed the story to me some days later, she still seemed unable to untangle what had happened.

As you know, Alice is a wonderful person but absolutely terrified (understandably) about memory loss — she's also very resistant to talking about it with me, and very good at hiding it when you see her for a quick coffee or chat on the phone. She would be upset if she knew I had emailed you — but I am worried and did want you to know.

With kind regards
Ella Longmire

Dear Ella
Thank you for your email. I understand the delicacy of the situation and will assess the issue diplomatically without involving you.

Regards
Professor Brewster.

On the day of my father's wake, it stormed. There was a portable air conditioner in every room of his small house and each one roared like a terrifying beast, emitting only a puny puff of cool air despite its bluster.

The air was still and the clouds were gathering, clotted and thick, as my half siblings tried to speak above the great rumble of those machines, praising a man I hadn't seen for many years but certainly didn't remember with the fondness they seemed to feel.

'Why don't they turn them off?' I muttered to Alice, who had insisted I come. 'It's not like they're making any difference.'

There were ninety of us crowded into those rooms, and each and every relative of my father's looked frighteningly familiar to me, despite the fact I knew so few of them. Tall and heavy-set, with wide hooded eyes, full lips, and a strong nose: *These are the Haldons*, I thought, *and I am one of them.*

Tom, my father's oldest son from his first marriage, was the only one with whom I had a relationship that came close to resembling family.

He'd been born to my father and his legitimate wife five months before my mother, who lived at the other end of the street to Mr and Mrs Haldon, went into labour with me — the other child, the secret one.

Sometimes my father would bring Tom with him when he came visiting, no doubt getting some kind of perverse thrill out of seeing us together, while his wife, Judith, was bemused at this out-of-character demonstration of fatherly care for their son.

So, I knew Tom, although I didn't know he was my brother until my mother spilled the whole sad and sorry story to me and Judith and everyone in the neighbourhood. It was my seventh birthday and we had spent hours with all the doors locked, waiting for the police. Outside, my father shouted at her to let him in. He threatened to burn the house down. *Alice*, he screamed. *Alice*.

The irritated constable who finally came reprimanded him and scolded my mother. The next morning she and I left the neighbourhood, stopping at every letterbox as we drove out, a handwritten card with the entire saga summarised, and an apology for the untoward noise, deposited (by me) in each slot.

When the thunder came it shook us all with its ferocity, a great shuddering of the bones accompanied by a crack of lightning and a sudden blast of wind. And then the rain. This was the third storm that week. Outside a tree fell, crashing onto the neighbour's fence, and everyone screamed.

'There's nothing we can do,' Tom called out. 'It's safer to stay inside.'

'It's Johannes,' someone laughed.

I looked at Alice and rolled my eyes. She scowled.

'No matter what you or I may think of him,' she had told me, 'he is your father and you need to honour his passing.'

She leant forward now, the veins in her hands blue and knotted as she gripped the arms of the chair. Sometimes she looked so frail it broke my heart.

'I don't like this climate change,' she said to me, her voice barely discernible above the lashing of the rain. 'They keep telling us about the impending disasters awaiting us, but what if we're already living it? What if it's happening now?'

When I visit the doctor, she asks me about my family history.

I've come to an age where I can no longer assume good health with the confidence I once had. She takes my blood pressure and it is high. She measures my cholesterol and it's above what it should be. I am always tired, I complain. More than tired. Sometimes so weary I can barely function. I worry I have some strange virus that cannot be detected but is breaking down my immune system piece by piece. I worry that we are all being attacked by this virus. That it's a product of what we are doing to the environment.

'One thing at a time,' she tells me.

She wants to know if high blood pressure and high cholesterol run in the family.

I tell her that Alice has always been well. She is eighty-four now and not nearly as strong as she once was, but this is to be expected. My concerns about her memory are the first real worries I have had about her health. I am not sure if she is taking any medication for blood pressure and cholesterol. I assume not. I've never known her to have any heart problems. There has, of course, been her neuropathy, which she seems to control with Lyrica. And I've told the neurologist about her increasing forgetfulness. Her mother had Alzheimer's, and *her* mother before that.

I am talking too much. It's all a jumble.

'Blood pressure? Cholesterol? So, both fine as far you know?'

I nod.

'What about your father?'

I look at her as though she has gone completely and utterly barmy. *What about him?* I think. He has had no role in my life so why would he have any relevance to my genetic make-up? A false assumption, I realise with a sickening thud.

'I have absolutely no idea,' I tell her.

Dear Professor Brewster

I know I have written to you already and I run the risk of seeming like one of those irritating, harassing relatives by writing to you again.

Alice mentioned that you discussed her memory when she saw you last and that you assured her she was doing fine. Unfortunately, I don't think this is the case. Last week she got lost when she drove to my house, despite having driven here so many times. She kept calling me on her mobile saying she didn't know where she was. I had to tell her to go to the nearest street corner and give me the names of each of the roads. I had to make her promise not to move until I came to get her. When I found her she was in tears.

I don't know what the ethics of this situation is, but I think she needs to be tested for Alzheimer's so that she can have the earliest possible intervention with medication.

I am trying to talk to her about this, but I do need the support of her doctors.

Regards
Ella.

Dear Ella

Thank you for your email expressing your concerns. They have been noted.

Regards
Professor Brewster.

In his will, my father leaves me his house.

It is enough to cause World War Three to break out between the Haldons and myself.

Alice tells me I have every right to it. 'He never provided for you,' she says. 'I never asked him to. But I shouldn't have had to. You're his daughter. And I will have nothing to leave you.'

It's true. She lives in a small, rented flat two suburbs away from me. Fortunately it's on the ground floor, because I don't think she could manage stairs anymore. And she has neighbours who like and care for her. People of all ages have always liked Alice. My friends go to visit her. They seek out her opinion and advice. They suggest I bring her with me when they invite me for dinner. There are times when I find it all too close, when I would like a little more separation from her, but I know that when she's gone, the void will be darker and deeper than the hole in the ozone layer. It is liable to swallow me whole for some time.

'I wonder what it's worth,' I say, completely bemused by the strange, unexpected nature of this inheritance that I already realise I won't be able to take without a fight.

'Two hundred dollars?' Alice guesses.

She isn't trying to be funny or silly. She has lost all grasp of numbers. Concepts like time, numbers on a digital clock have gone, slipped away like a shed skin.

'I'm seeing you tomorrow morning,' I might tell her.

'So when's that?' she will ask.

'The day after today. Lunch, dinner, sleep, and then you wake up and it's tomorrow.'

'So I will see you soon then. What would you like?'

'What do you mean?'

'For dinner.'

I am trying not to get too frustrated — but it isn't easy. There are bad days when I have to go through the day, the date, the time with her over and over again. There are mornings at work when she rings me at least four times, wanting me to clarify, just quickly, whether she has coffee with her friend, Diane, today or tomorrow. And then, if I tell her I am anxious about her memory, she becomes cranky. She didn't sleep well, she says. She forgot to write the appointment down. She hasn't called four times. Really, I do exaggerate.

Tom is the envoy sent to approach me about the house. He telephones, full of good cheer, the boom of his voice not dissimilar to my memory of my father's.

Of course Johannes should have provided for me, he says, they all agree on that. But as the house is the principal asset, and likely to be worth a couple of million, it seems a little extreme. A little unfair. The rest of them are left with a few worthless stocks and bonds, an ancient Rover, a cellar full of red wine, and some very average art. To be split between seven. Which doesn't amount to much.

I ask him what his suggestion is.

'Well,' and he sounds a little more hesitant here, 'we include the house with all the assets to be split, and you receive a share of the total, commensurate with your relationship to him.'

'Commensurate with my relationship to him?'

'It's not like you ever lived with him,' he says, even more hesitation in his tone. 'It's not like you were his child. His real child, that is.'

The hesitation is sliding now towards the turning point, the tip-over into anger.

'And if I don't agree?'

'The others want to take the will to the courts. To challenge it.'

I tell him to go for it.

And they do. Three days later, I am contacted by the lawyer on behalf of the estate. I am told that the assets are frozen, and that the other named beneficiaries have filed a petition in court.

Alice is suitably furious on my behalf. She tells me that I should stand up for myself.

'I'm proud of you,' she says. 'You need the money and he owes you. You're never going to earn much working for that political organisation.'

'Greenpeace,' I remind her.

'You won't ever own a house,' she says. 'And being old with no assets, well …' She shrugs. 'It's a little like living on the edge of a cliff.'

She wants to document the amount that Johannes

never paid — the costs of feeding, clothing, educating me.

'Complete with CPI and inflation?'

She does her best not to look too befuddled at this, a scrap of paper on the table in front of her as she starts writing down figures. I am exhausted at the prospect.

'I think I might need a lawyer,' I tell her.

Outside the heat is unbearable, the sky thick with smoke from the surrounding bushfires, ash on the air, charred to the tongue. The news is running twenty-four hours with updates on the encroaching flames, some of the outer suburbs already evacuated. I have closed all the windows and doors, and turned on each of Alice's fans, and they churn sluggishly. I suggest setting up some Coolgardie safes — stringing wet towels around the room to cool us. She is focusing on her nonsensical numbers so doesn't answer, and I go to the linen cupboard.

The scrap of paper is at the bottom — an appointment with a neuropsychologist. The date: a week ago.

Alice feigns confusion. Or perhaps she isn't feigning, perhaps she genuinely forgot, or didn't think the appointment was for her — although who she thought it *was* for is difficult to fathom.

'So you didn't go?'

'How could I have?' she asks. 'I didn't even know it was on.'

Dear Professor Brewster

I understand you referred my mother to Vera Smythe. As you may be aware, she missed the appointment.

I have made another time for her, the week before she is due to see you next. She has agreed that I can go with her to both appointments. I hope this is alright with you.

Yours sincerely

Ella Longmire.

If your mother is happy for you to come, I have no objections.

Professor Brewster.

It takes a week to bring the bushfires under control. Two suburbs are burnt to the ground; charred remains of houses feature on the news, along with stories of heroic dogs and laconic homeowners who shrug at the camera and say: 'What can you do? Crack a tinnie and clean up, I guess.'

The fires are followed by days of torrential rain and an outbreak of a strange virus causing a rash on small children across the city.

If I didn't work in media relations, I'd turn everything off — computers, phones, radios, televisions.

Gretchen, Tom's wife, rings me late at night to scream at me. Tom has lost his job and they can no longer afford their daughter's school fees. She was relying on their share of the house. How dare I?

Sarah, Tom's sister, tells me they are fast losing sympathy for me. What do I need money for? It's not like I have any children to provide for.

Tom tries to cajole me. The lawyers' fees will eat up a huge portion of the estate. Surely we can come to an arrangement?

Alice's neighbour calls. She found her out on the street in her pyjamas at four am. Drenched to the skin she was. Drenched to the skin.

Dear Professor Brewster
The world is going to hell in a handbasket.
    Ella

Professor Brewster takes my mother's arm and leads her gently to a seat. She introduces him to me and he shakes my hand, cool, dry skin, without meeting my gaze.

He has the results of Alice's tests with the neuropsychologist, several sheafs of paper, in front of him. He shifts them to one side. His desk is covered with books, articles, piles and piles of paper, seemingly left in no order. His shelves are overflowing with texts and journals, stuffed into every available space. He looks across at Alice and for a moment, I think he is a little like Andy Warhol, smooth skin and a shock of white hair.

'Well,' he says, and his voice is soft. 'I'm afraid the results aren't good.'

I glance at her, but her eyes are turned towards him.

'Oh.' It is the only word she utters.

'As you know, the test is broad ranging — covering memory, capacity to focus on a task, capacity to follow a logical progression, and so on. And the results are calibrated according to your education and professional background. We also bear in mind the stress of the test itself.'

Cut to the chase, I think, but when I glance at Alice again, I can see she isn't wanting him to get to the end result. She is listening carefully, leaning forward slightly.

'I was having a bad day,' she tells him. 'I hadn't slept very well.'

'Still,' he says softly, 'I'm afraid the results in all areas were not good.'

She nods, gaze now fixed on her hands.

It seems she has Alzheimer's. The patterns point strongly in that direction.

'But you don't know for sure?' she asks.

He smiles. 'There are further tests we can do, but the indications are such that I'm not sure they'll be worth your while.'

I take Alice's hand in my own, each bone brittle like a bird's.

'Is there anything I can do — to fix it?' she asks.

'No,' I whisper, and across the desk from me, Professor Brewster is shaking his head.

'But we can try and slow it down,' he says. 'There are drugs that do have some effect. You have to qualify, and we trial you on them for six months. If the results are positive, you'll continue to get them under the PBS.'

'How do I qualify?'

She needs to do another memory test, just a simple one, here with him, and if her results are low enough, he can start her immediately.

She sits bolt upright, ready. 'Well, let's do it,' she tells him.

'Are you sure you want to do it now?' I ask.

She nods.

He has the questions on a form. What day of the week is it? What month? The year? The season? I am going to say three words to you: apple, pen and cup. At the end of the test I will ask you to repeat these to me. Count from a hundred backwards in multiples of seven. Spell 'world' backwards. I'm going to show you a shape and I want you to copy it on this piece of paper. And now, the three words, can you repeat them?

I listen as Alice answers all the questions, apart from the three words and copying the shape, correctly. I'm astounded.

Professor Brewster shakes his head. 'I'm afraid you did too well,' he says.

Alice looks confused.

'We wanted you to do badly, so you could get the drug,' I explain.

Still she doesn't understand.

Then I glance down to see that she has answers written on the skin just above her knee — the date, the multiples of seven, even 'world' spelt backwards. She knows the questions they ask — from her visit to the neuropsychologist, probably earlier visits with him, perhaps even the GP. And I know she has been asking her friends about common memory questions, no doubt taking notes.

'You weren't meant to cheat.' I laugh feebly and point at her leg.

Professor Brewster shakes his head, his smile slight as he ticks the box that says she's eligible, and for the first time, I smile back at him.

* * *

Tom and I are the only two at the mediation.

We shake hands and he cannot look me in the eye. His skin is dry and flaky, his face covered with a fine red rash, and I wonder whether he has caught the virus that has been in the news, although I had assumed it only affected children.

'You don't look well,' I tell him and he flinches slightly.

The mediator explains the process to us — Tom has been appointed to represent the wishes of all of Johannes' children.

'Except me,' I add.

She nods. 'Of course.'

We each have time to speak, to explain our perspective on the dispute and to outline what we want and why. The aim of the process is to find a solution that we both feel we can agree to.

Two hours later we leave with nothing resolved.

In the lift Tom asks me why I am being so intransient. I resist the urge to ask the same of him. Instead I tell him that I feel I am in the right.

'He never gave me or Alice anything. This is reparation.'

He doesn't reply.

'Besides,' I add. 'I need the money.'

That night I pick up Alice and we drive out to Johannes' house. I haven't been there since the funeral.

The tree is still lying across the yard, the fence crushed beneath its weight, and I have to take Alice's hand and guide her carefully in the darkness. We sit on the back verandah and look down to the harbour in the distance, the reflection of the lights shivering in the oily water.

'Did you love him?' I ask Alice.

She doesn't reply immediately but when she does, she is, as she usually is, surprisingly lucid in discussing emotions. 'I was young. He was older and handsome. I was bored. It was thrilling. It wasn't until I had you that I grew up, and I realised that what we had wasn't love, nor was it exciting. But I was caught. He was your father, even if he didn't behave like one, so I wasn't as hard on him as early as I should have been.'

She closes her eyes for a moment.

'He wrote to me before he died. He told me he was sorry for how he treated us both, you in particular. He said he wanted to make up for it. I suppose that's why he left you the house.'

I ask her if she still has the letter. 'It could be useful,' I say.

She isn't sure.

'I thought we could live here,' I tell her.

She shakes her head. 'I have Alzheimer's,' she tells me. 'Caring for me will get too difficult.'

Lightning flashes out on the harbour, a silver slash, followed moments later by a deep rumble of thunder.

'Maybe it always storms here,' Alice says, and she looks at me, querying whether this is possible.

'Perhaps,' I say.

* * *

The next night, Timothy, one of my father's other sons, calls me.

'A neighbour reported that you were at my father's house,' he says. 'What right do you have? What right?'

I hang up on him.

Dear Professor Brewster

How much longer do I have with my mother?

   Ella

A month before the hearing is due to commence, Tom is admitted to hospital.

Alice and I are having a coffee, sitting by the window that overlooks the emergency drop off, when I see Gretchen at the cafeteria fridge. She is holding the door open, unable to make her selection, a tin of iced tea in one hand.

'The world is dying because of people like you,' the customer behind her says. 'You act as though we have endless energy to burn. Iced tea or juice? Iced tea or juice? There won't be either when you've finished contributing to global warming.'

'Oh fuck off,' Gretchen says and slams the door shut.

It is Alice who approaches her, who asks her why she's here. I don't dare.

Gretchen tells her that Tom was admitted last night. He cannot breathe without a respirator, he has lost all feeling in his limbs, and his entire body is covered in the rash. The doctors don't know why, she says.

She is crying as she speaks, and I watch in surprise as Alice hugs her.

'I'm scared he's not going to make it.' Gretchen's sob is deep, guttural, enough to make the woman at the table closest to her gulp her tea a little too loudly.

I am scared he won't want to see us, but Alice tells me not to be ridiculous.

'You played together as children. There's been enough fighting. It's time to put it to one side.'

When Gretchen asks why we are here, Alice looks at

her directly. 'I'm seeing my neurologist,' she says. 'I have Alzheimer's.'

Her answer is so crisp and clear it is difficult to believe that there is anything wrong with her, but only moments earlier, she had asked me, once again, if I remembered when she, Alice, was a baby, unable to comprehend that this was an impossibility.

'Oh dear,' Gretchen says, but I can tell she hasn't really listened, her mind is on Tom. Alice is old, and old people always have something wrong with them.

Tom is asleep when we go to his room. His daughter is sitting with him. I can see she is apprehensive about my presence, but Alice assures her we are just here to send our love and wish him all the best. She goes over to Tom's bed and takes his hand, stroking it for a moment.

'He's lucky to have you here,' she tells his daughter.

'If I can get you anything,' I say uselessly to Gretchen as we leave.

She doesn't even look up.

'Now what am I going to do about the court case?' I ask Alice. 'I feel like a terrible heel if I keep going.'

'What court case?' she asks, her eyes clouded again, her hand tight on my arm as she asks me to walk a little more slowly. 'Where are we going? Home?'

A week later my lawyer calls with a settlement offer. I am to get a quarter of the estate, with the rest of Johannes' children to split the remainder between them.

'I would advise you to take it,' she says. 'There's no guarantee you'll get any better if we went to trial, and the costs would be significant.'

I tell her I need a little time to think, and she says they have given me twenty-four hours.

I am at work, a report detailing the rise in catastrophic weather events in front of me, numbers ready to be distilled into a press release that no one will want to read. Outside the day is perfect: warm and still, the sky a sharp turquoise.

I wish I could talk to Alice about the offer, but I know the numbers would not make sense to her, and if it was a bad day, she would not even know what the court case was about or why I was in dispute with my half-siblings, and then she would become anxious. She worries now, picking like a small bird at each possibility — what happens if she is not home when the meals I have arranged for her arrive, what will she do with the food she buys for herself if there is not enough room in the fridge, what if she puts the heavy blanket on the bed and it is hot, does she have a heart problem if she finds it difficult to breathe, who will look after her cat when she dies?

I am exhausted.

I call the lawyer back ten minutes later and tell her I will take their offer.

'You've made the right decision,' she says. 'I'll let you know when all the papers are ready to sign.'

* * *

I text Gretchen to find out how Tom is, and she replies with two words only: *the same*.

I send another feeble message offering generic help if she needs anything, knowing she won't call on me.

They all hate me, but it's not as though they were ever really my friends, let alone family. It's not as though I've lost anything concrete — only the possibility of a relationship with them, and perhaps that possibility hasn't even been lost, only diminished. And did I really want that anyway? I don't know. But I do know that on the bad days with Alice, I wish I had brothers and sisters, a father, even cousins.

'Why did you never meet anyone else?' I ask her.

She tells me she was too busy working and looking after me. There is no accusation in her tone nor a desire to incite guilt, not even when she goes on to remind me that she was a single mother, without much support.

'There were a couple of men,' she says wistfully. 'But I don't think they were keen on taking on a child.'

She asks me what I intend to do with the $500 I inherited from Johannes.

I don't correct her as to the amount.

Once I would have liked to buy somewhere to live, somewhere far away where the air is clean and I could grow food and pretend that the world isn't crumbling around me. But life has changed. I will need the money for Alice's care.

'Buy a house,' I tell her. 'Invest it wisely. Put a little aside for fun.' I list everything I think she wants to hear, expecting her to nod in agreement, but instead she just turns to the television and switches it on, the sound of the dialogue drowning out my voice, her eyes fixed on the screen.

This is what she does now, disappears; usually just for a few minutes, but often enough to make me realise we are at the beginning of a very long farewell. I put a blanket around her and clear our dinner plates, washing up under the dim light of her kitchen.

Dear Professor Brewster

Is it inevitable that Alice will go into a home? And if it is, how will I know when it's time?

We are gradually getting used to things she can no longer do for herself, basic tasks such as cooking and cleaning and even showering slowly slipping away. Sleep now seems to be going. I think she lies awake most nights. Sometimes she gets up and walks the streets, and then she complains of how tired she is during the day, wanting only to nap.

I have heard that people with Alzheimer's often become incontinent, or is that they forget to go to the toilet when they need to? I'm not sure, and it doesn't really matter. But when does all this add up to enough, when is it neglect to leave her at home on her own?

She tells me she can't bear the thought of leaving her flat, of going to a place where she will wait to die. And so I leave her there but I feel so guilty, that I am being a bad daughter. Is there a line that you can identify for me, a place that you can say: *okay, now we are here, it's time?*

I know you won't answer me, we seem to have moved way past that point, even I'm aware of this.

So why do I write?

I need to think about that.

Ella

The time comes with more clarity than I expect.

In the middle of the night, one of Alice's neighbours calls to tell me she fell in the garden. He has rung an ambulance and she is on her way to emergency.

The television screens in the hospital show the floods in Queensland, rising waters the colour of old coffee swirling and lapping as rivers burst their banks and rush down streets; furniture, clothing, garden equipment, all detritus now, swept up in the filthy flow. Standing in a yellow raincoat an old woman sobs: 'I can't take it anymore,' she says.

Alice is in a bed, her skin the colour of dirty paper, her eyes closed. In her hand she has a morphine button, which she is meant to push when the pain becomes too much. I'm not sure if she understood the instructions, but as she does not seem to be grimacing, I assume she has been dosing herself.

Apparently she has hit her head, and blood needs to be drained from her brain.

'She has Alzheimer's,' I tell anyone who will listen, and there aren't many who are all that keen.

The surgeon is younger than I am, and he has little patience with my concerns as I nudge at the larger question — should we be operating? If we don't, what are the ramifications? Would she die or would she just continue to live with both dementia and brain damage from the fall?

Somebody help me, I whisper to myself in the

bathroom. *I can't do this on my own.*

And then I remember that I have his mobile number.

Dear Professor Brewster,

I know I have been writing to you more than I should but Alice has had a fall and is about to operated on. I would really appreciate your advice.

    Ella.

'He's coming,' I tell Alice. 'He'll help us,' I say.

But of course he doesn't, and I can only watch as they wheel her into theatre, knowing I have been unable to ask what needed to be asked, let alone say that this is it: the end of the line.

And so, when he does arrive, the deed is done. The blood has been drained, and with it we have lost much of her. She does not know us, or even herself, and he tells me he is very sorry it has come to this.

'She was doing so well,' he says.

I just nod.

And then I cannot help myself, I start to cry, and as I do so, I tell him that this is what she was always terrified of, and I failed to protect her. 'Her mother had Alzheimer's,' I say. 'And her grandmother. She saw them both end up completely gaga. She told me to put a pillow over her head if she was ever diagnosed.' I shake my head. 'And to never let her end up in a nursing home. I've broken both promises now.'

He remains by the door, awkward and silent, waiting for me to finish.

At least I have the money to find her a moderately decent place, I think.

I tell him that I promise not to write anymore. I apologise if I've crossed a line with my letters.

He smiles at me, gently now, kinder than I have seen him be. Behind him the rain lashes at the windows, the wind howls, and the world is once again going to hell in a handbasket.

'But can I ask you one more question?' Not that he's answered any of my others, I think. 'Can you see Alzheimer's before it's evident? I read you could. Up to twenty years before there are any signs.'

He nods.

'So it could be in there now?' I tap at my skull.

'It could be,' he says. He turns to look out the window for a moment. 'But I'm not sure what point there is in detecting catastrophe long before it eventuates. Unless there is a sure means of diverting it. Besides anything could happen in the meantime. Anything at all.'

And so there it is, I think as I kiss Alice goodbye.

'I'll be back to see you in the morning,' I say, but she doesn't even register me.

She's gone, I think, and I am right behind her marching towards a line I won't know how to recognise. And do I really want to know? Do we ever want to know? Even when the truth is so close as to be incontrovertible, we frequently do our best to look the other way, hoping, hoping that this isn't happening, we're not living it already, and that tomorrow will continue to dawn, another day: clear, sweet, and unremarkable.

FAR FROM HOME

High in the hills it was still too hot, although from the back of an air-conditioned car you could almost pretend that it was a European winter, the clouds were so grey and low.

In the front seat, her mother asked Ketuk, the driver, the same questions over and over again, mostly innocuous variations of where he was born, or some harmless query about what they were passing. Then, whenever there was a pause, she would lean over to ask whether they had bushfires in these hills.

This last one didn't make sense to him.

'Yeeeees,' he said, drawing the word out like a wide uncertain smile, although it was clear he didn't understand her.

'This is your lunch hotel,' he said with some relief, as

he turned down a narrow drive, bamboo pressing close on either side.

Sione had expected something a little grander, but then the ridiculously expensive was often strangely ordinary, she thought — how lavish could you go before you were just treading water and fiddling with the finer details?

The driver gave her a card.

'When you finish lunch, they will call me,' he told her.

In the driveway, an old man swept up dried husks from the palms, long-dead leaves from the frangipanis, and brown, bruised blossoms. The slow steady brush of straw was a soothing and familiar rhythm underneath the rapid trickle of water from the fountain.

Each morning, in their own hotel by the coast, Sione had woken to this sound: the detritus of the night swept up, the gentle rush of the brooms along the pathways that bordered the gardens around their bungalows. It was always old men sweeping; dressed in dark green trousers and shirts, they would stop in their task and smile at her as she walked down to the seaside promenade before breakfast.

Here the man was also dressed in the same green, but he did not look up; his eyes remained focused on the ground as they were shown in the direction of the restaurant. She took her mother's hand, the frailness of her wrist and the bruisings on her skin perpetually disarming.

'Slowly,' she said as they approached the stairs, smooth, shiny tiles that were bound to be slippery. 'Take the railing.'

'I'd like to go to the bathroom,' her mother said, insisting that she could manage on her own.

And Sione let her, partly because it was always a matter of flip-flopping around on the line that divided holding onto some semblance of independence for her mother, and recognising that this was foolish. But the truth was, she was also eager to have any chance to get away from her.

'I wish you were here,' she'd told Louis last night. 'I get so fed up and then I feel so guilty. I know I'm meant to just agree with everything she says, no matter how wrong it is — yes it's breakfast time, even though it's clearly night, sure a backless halterneck would look good on a ninety-year-old — but I just can't do it.'

'Ah well,' he said. 'If she wants to flash her back, let her.'

'When I said I didn't think the dress would work on her, that backless was a little inappropriate, she said no one saw her back anymore. Which I suppose was her thinking that because she didn't see it, no one else did.'

'Maybe it's a spectacular back,' he offered.

She was drunk when she called him. She was often drunk soon after her mother went to sleep. Not that it took much. Two Bintangs by the pool and she veered rapidly from alcohol-induced elation to guilt, sorrow, and missing him and home.

Now, as she hovered outside the toilet and peered into the window of the hotel gift shop, she was becoming anxious. After ten minutes, Sione decided she needed to check.

'Are you alright?' she called as she pushed the door open.

'No,' her mother replied.

She was looking up at her from the floor, her face white, another bruise already swelling, and Sione, being hopeless in any kind of crisis, just screamed.

The hotel didn't have a doctor, but her mother insisted she was fine. It was just a shock; she hadn't cut herself or broken anything, she just needed to lie down for a little while. Sione should have lunch, and then they would return to the coast, where she could go to the hospital if she didn't feel better.

Out on the verandah, Sione sat under a fan, the slow *tick tick* overhead bringing with it the faintest puff of breeze. She could see rice paddies, terraces of fragile green under an oppressive sky, and below that the hotel pool, an aquamarine that spilt over the horizon, glassy in the sharp light of the building storm.

The table behind her was full of Americans. She hadn't really taken them in when she was shown her seat. Two men and a woman, all dressed in white and either pale pink or lemon, speaking loudly of someone in the movies, someone whose career was imploding because of her unfortunate move to Texas. They seemed to be about sixty, although one of the men was younger, olive-skinned and handsome, his accent not as pronounced.

Next to her was a French family: a mother, grandmother, and two sons fighting over an iPad. The boys ordered burgers and fries. The women, both of whom seemed fresh from Botox treatments, had tea only.

And then there was the honeymoon couple.

Sione glanced across at them as she ordered a soto ayam — not quite sure why she wanted soup in this heat, but perhaps it was the comfort factor. The young woman kept taking photos of her meal on a phone that was so overburdened with gold accessories it was a wonder she could hold it up.

Standing at the edge of the balcony, Sione looked down at the pool. Its smooth surface was disturbed by one old man slowly doing breaststroke in a diagonal, the gentle plod of his strokes discernible in the hushed stillness. By the edge, his two tanned daughters (she presumed and then hoped that's what they were) stretched out on sun lounges.

When she sat down again, the Americans were leaving.

The more handsome of the party seemed to think he knew her.

'Sione?'

She nodded, desperately trying to place his face.

'Michael. Michael Pavlou.'

And as he uttered his name, she blushed, hating herself for doing so.

She'd been fifteen, staying overnight at her friend Marina's. Marina was a new friend — smart, funny, pretty, one of those sporty, clever, popular girls — a trifecta that invariably led to physiotherapy. Michael was her older brother. He was studying law, she remembered. And he had a girlfriend, a slightly pimply Greek girl, who was also a law student and whose clothes weren't quite in fashion. The four of them had been watching television and then Karla, the girlfriend, had gone home.

Lying in the dark, she and Marina had talked as teenage girls did — about school work, friends, movies, and perhaps even a little about Michael and Karla. Sione had thought he was handsome. She didn't understand why he was with Karla.

Later, as she hovered on the edge of sleep, Marina's breathing steady and slow in the bed next to her, the whole house still, there was a tap on the door.

'Shh,' Michael told her, beckoning for her to follow him.

His room was at the end of the corridor, his bed unmade, the smell of him, sweet and musty, the sheets still warm from where he'd been lying, the curtains slightly open to the frosty spill of the moon.

Sione had never even kissed a boy.

But she got into bed with him, and she followed each

and every one of his instructions to the letter — a rapid sex education, which would have been more enjoyable if he'd been a little less insistent about what he wanted and how.

Perhaps he would have moved beyond the urgency of his own needs if his mother hadn't almost caught them. She would never know. Mrs Pavlou opened the door to his room and he'd pushed her down under the doona with such force that she'd wondered whether she was going to be able to breathe. About five minutes after she left, Marina came in and told her she had to get back to their room — 'now'.

'Mum's wondering where you are.'

And she had pulled her nightie back down and run, as quietly as she could, sliding back into the trundle bed moments before Mrs Pavlou looked in.

She'd been obsessed with Michael, but at least had the sense not to talk about it too much to Marina.

'He has a girlfriend, you know.' It was Marina's only comment to her on the matter.

And then she had, embarrassingly, got very drunk at a party and cried, telling Marina she loved him and he'd used her, and she hadn't had her period (the last bit was a lie).

Marina was a good girl. She became school captain the following year and was only four marks off being dux. She must have told Michael to ring her, which he did — his words kind but firm as soon as he realised she wasn't pregnant.

'You're too young for me,' he'd said. 'I'm with Karla,' he'd told her. 'I'm sorry I hurt you.'

She hadn't cried. But her voice had squeaked a little when she'd said she was fine, she hadn't even given him a thought, there was no need for him to worry, and she hoped he and Karla would be very happy together.

Now as she looked at him, she wondered whether she would have recognised him if he hadn't told her who he was. He wasn't as handsome as she'd first thought. It was really no more than a mass of features she thought of as appealing — dark skin, white teeth, dark eyes — but there was something of the ferret to him, she realised. There probably always had been.

'What are you doing here?' he asked.

The waiter placed her chicken soup in front of her as she explained she was just here for lunch with her mother, who'd had a fall and was resting, which was why she was eating alone.

He'd come on a holiday.

'Not the one I'd expected,' he told her, as he pulled out a seat, stretching his tanned legs out in front of him.

She had a slice of bread left and he helped himself, dipping it in the last of the oil. For a moment she imagined telling him she'd been saving that for her soup, but then decided it would be simpler (and more mature) to call the waiter and ask for more.

'Divorce,' Michael told her. 'Or at least staring down the barrel of it. She left me a week before we were due to come here. I came anyway.'

'It's a beautiful place,' she replied, wondering why he'd chosen to sit with her when she hadn't requested his company.

The dark clouds were pressing low and the deep boom of thunder promised a heavy downpour. Overhead the fan continued to tick, pushing thick sluggish air around with little effect.

She asked him what he did now, where he was living, looking across at him as she spoke.

He was a sports agent in LA. He'd been there for close to twenty years. He leant back in his chair and waved a napkin in front of his face.

If she'd held any illusion that he was going to ask her about herself, she didn't hold it for long. He was simply sitting there, no doubt willing to answer her next question if she had one, but other than that, his contribution to the conversation wasn't going to amount to much.

'So what are the rooms like here?' She regretted the words as soon as she uttered them, dismayed by the thought that he might think she was cracking onto him, and she shook her head slightly, grinning as she did so.

'Sorry,' she told him, aware that the heat and her embarrassment were only going to make her blunder further. 'I'm not cracking onto you for old time's sake. I was just curious as to what you'd get for such a large sum of money.' Now she was commenting on his wealth, she thought, but fuck it — she'd seen the small suburban house he'd come from, the room with the Kmart doona cover and faded striped curtains.

His laughter was a relief. 'I haven't heard that expression for years.' And then he stood. 'I'll show you,' he told her. 'And I'm not cracking onto you either. Or at least I'm not planning on it right at this minute.'

The bungalow opened onto a garden, each wall seeming to slide back to let in the cool green. The room itself was relatively simple: the floors stone, the furniture teak, a palatial bed in the centre, a throne beneath the wafting white mosquito netting. He took her through to a sitting area that also opened onto a stretch of impossible emerald lawn, and beyond that a pool, which he told her he shared with three other garden suites.

'Top of the range have their own pools,' he said. 'My friends at lunch have one of those. He's a very successful producer.'

'And she's?'

He shrugged. 'His wife.'

She told him it was beautiful.

She should probably get back to her mother, and as she spoke he stepped a little closer, the slight sweetness to his sweat familiar, a glint in his eyes as he smiled.

'What's the hurry?' he asked. 'Someone will come and get you if she wakes or needs you.'

'But no one knows I'm here.'

He shook his head. 'They know, believe me,' he said. 'This is a place where they know — everything you could ever want or need. Before you even know it.'

The heat and the absurdity of the situation made her laugh, the sound more nervous than her usual throaty laughter, more of an uncomfortable squawk as she began to fend him off, putting one arm on his shoulder and stepping back.

'You *are* trying to crack onto me,' she protested. 'God knows why.' She told him she was in a relationship. She was faithful. She wasn't here for this, she was just on a terrible holiday with her mother who had dementia, and coming here had been a way of trying to pass another day because it was hell sitting by the pool in an endless circle of the same conversation with a woman who'd once been so alive and intelligent and was disappearing before her eyes.

'And maybe a quick fuck with the man that I lost my virginity to would pass a little more time and be part of this entire absurd package, but I'm not up for it,' she said.

He stopped then.

All the swagger in his posture seemed to sag. He sat, legs crossed in front of him, and put his head in his hands.

It took her a moment before she realised his shoulders were shaking, and she knelt on the floor next to him, one arm on his, and told him it was okay, although she had no idea what 'it' was, other than a single word in an empty attempt at consolation.

He lifted his head and looked at her.

Later she wondered why she leant forward and kissed

him, but it was only a brief moment of wondering because she knew it for what it was, both at the time and afterwards. Neither of them spoke and she felt him hesitantly following her lead, a drowning man holding onto a drowning woman as they each tried to swim back up towards the surface.

When the rain fell it was torrential, so loud that even if one of them had chosen to speak, it would have been difficult to hear the other. She was glad of it, all of her intensely focused on his body and her own. She would forget this, as soon as it was over. She would say nothing of it to Louis, to anyone. It was just right here, now, and when they finally shifted away from each other, the heat unbearable, she allowed herself to look at him again.

'Are you married?' he asked her.

She nodded.

'Children?'

She shook her head.

'Did you want them?'

The question disarmed her. She had wanted them. Terribly. But Louis hadn't. And so eventually she had come to convince herself that she hadn't really. And now here she was, just beyond the possibility of it ever happening, even by accident, both feet firmly in a future that did not hold any chance of her stepping over into that other land, the one where she had assumed she would live.

'And you?'

He told her he had twins, boys, eight years old.

'They'll live with you both?' she asked.

He was sitting up in the bed, looking out at the garden. The rain had stopped, but each of the leaves, the grass, the heavy clusters of frangipani, the tall stems of ginger, the moss that grew in the stone wall, all of it was shining, the weight of that downpour still heavy on every leaf and petal.

The knock on the door was soft, the voice only just loud enough to be heard. 'Excuse me, madam. Madam.'

She stood up, quickly dressing herself as she said she would be right out.

He was waiting for her, the man who had met her and her mother at reception, and behind him another man, both with parasols protecting them from the last of the rain, both looking at her, solicitous, apprehensive.

'Has something happened?' she asked.

She could sense Michael behind her, his arm holding her up, as they told her it was her mother.

'I am very sorry, madam. We do not know what happened …'

She must have held on to him because he stopped her from falling, the rush of green coming up towards her as he scooped her up, holding her steady as they hurried back across that garden, past the smooth surface of that pool, empty now, along the white tiled walkway, the old man still sweeping, and towards the room where they had put her mother to rest, and where she had died, alone.

* * *

The manager of the hotel took charge.

Sitting opposite him in his office, she tried to take in his words, but all she could hear was the trickle of the fountain outside and the slow brush of the broom; the old man still clearing up the debris from the afternoon storm.

A doctor would arrange for her mother's body to be taken to the morgue in Denpasar. She would need to speak to the insurance company about getting her flown back to Australia.

'Should I go with her?' she asked the manager, wanting someone to tell her what to do.

If she liked, it could be arranged. They would call her driver.

It was Michael who stopped her.

'Stay,' he insisted. 'You don't want to be alone. You can head down there tomorrow.'

Sitting out in the garden, she called Louis, leaving a message for him to get back to her — 'Something terrible has happened' — because she felt she couldn't say over the phone that her mother had died, she couldn't leave those words disembodied in a voicemail. And then she called straight back, not wanting to alarm him, but to say that it wasn't to her, the terrible thing hadn't happened to her, even though it had. And so, of course, she ended up phoning again, her words bald this time. 'It's Dora. She's died.'

'Can I have a drink?' she asked Michael.

He picked up the phone and ordered gin and tonic.

She was relieved to see it was a whole bottle, and a bucket of ice.

He poured them each a glass. 'I haven't drunk since my first year in LA.' He closed his eyes as he swallowed.

She downed hers quickly, pouring another immediately.

They would have been fucking as her mother had died. She could barely bring herself to look at him, but after her third glass the gap between being in bed with him and sitting here now began to disappear. She knew him, she thought. She really knew him. And he knew her.

She was pissed.

'I'm sorry about when I was fifteen. Pretending to be pregnant.' She shook her head as she uttered the words. 'It was a very bad thing to do.'

His swagger had returned. He sat back, legs slightly apart, and paid her apology little heed.

'And it was bad to Marina. She must have felt strange knowing I'd run off into your room and had sex with you and that your mother almost caught us. Let alone telling her I thought I was pregnant. No wonder she didn't want to be my friend afterwards.'

The sky had cleared again. The late afternoon heat was unbearable and she stood now, unsteady on her feet, and looked at the pool. She didn't say anything to him as she walked towards it, stepping in to her knees at first and then thinking why not? Why not go all the way in? What does it matter? What does anything matter today?

And so she submerged herself, the cool glassy turquoise enveloping her as she cried momentarily, her clothes clinging to her body and then floating upwards as she tried to sit on the bottom.

He gave her a towel when she emerged.

She was about to pour herself another drink when she realised she could be sick. 'I think I may need to eat,' she told him.

Again, he picked up the phone and ordered for her.

'It's so sad.' Her voice was softer now. 'For the last year, I have willed her to die. It's been excruciating. Everything was scrambled. Sometimes she would ring me eight, ten times in the morning, wanting to know what day it was, what time, when would I come and see her? Always insisting that her memory was still alright. And if I questioned her on how she managed anything — her medication, her money, turning off heaters, any of it, she would get so angry with me. And then there would be days when I would glimpse *her* again, and I would feel confused. I would think that maybe she was alright and I'd just imagined it. And I hated the way I was forgetting all the other versions of her. I'd loved her as a child. She was gentle to me, kind, and she smelt so good. I used to love borrowing her clothes, putting on her sweater and smelling her as I pulled it over my head. It was like sunshine on a tree trunk — warm, solid, real. And she made mistakes, but who doesn't? Oh, Jesus. Look at me here now. I should get home. I should get back to Louis.'

The sun was in her eyes when she looked over to him. She wanted to see him as she had when she was fifteen, when they'd sat in Marina's lounge room watching television and she'd been so aware of him sitting that little bit closer than he should.

She'd known he'd come and get her later. Or at least she'd hoped for it so fervently that it hadn't been a surprise when she'd heard his knock on the door.

She reached out and touched the side of his face.

'Are you going to kiss me again?' he asked.

She shook her head. 'Too drunk.'

'I'm sorry too.'

She realised then that he was on his third glass. His eyes had softened, the darkness of the iris covered by a slight haze of gin and heat.

She looked at the hairs on the back of his wrist and then down to his calves, his feet bare in the lush green grass.

'I was just a boy. We don't think like women.' His grin was rueful. 'Marina had the shits with me. Karla knew too. Or at least she guessed and I denied, convincingly enough to make her forgive me until I did it again with someone else.'

Sione's phone rang and she silenced it. It would be Louis. She didn't want to speak to him, not right then.

She looked across at Michael and smiled as she held

her glass up, the condensation glittering in the sunshine.

'Here's to Dora,' she said.

He clinked.

'And to me.'

He raised his glass again, eyes still on her. 'To what we once were and will become.'

She lay down on the grass, the low clouds spinning. 'And to what we are now.' She looked through the glass at him, each feature distorted, before she closed her eyes. 'Fucked, and far from home.'

LAST DAYS

In August, when the winds come, Annie looks out across the small garden and imagines living elsewhere. Golden-yellow puffs of wattle drift down, covering the bricks on the back patio, the patch of lawn, and the few sad vegetables in pots.

'It's wattle season again,' she tells Lou, who turns to her, momentarily bemused.

She is playing with her fuzzy felts on the back table, but she stands up now, tucking her small hands into her armpits and wiggling her bottom as she begins to quack.

Annie shakes her head and smiles. 'Why the duck?' she asks.

'Waddle season,' Lou tells her, and she returns to the felts.

'Ah.' Annie picks up a handful of yellow and holds it

out. 'Wattle,' she says. 'It's a flower.'

She feels too flat to laugh now, but she knows that later she will do so. She will probably relay the misunderstanding over dinner. Kath will be pouring wine, and she'll wonder why Annie hadn't told her this cute story earlier. Jane and Sara, who are also pregnant to the same donor Kath used, will find it amusing, and if Annie has had a few glasses already, she might even waddle herself.

She shakes her head.

'I think too much,' she tells Lou. 'Actually I think too little. That's the real problem.'

She stands out in the garden and raises her face to the sky, breathing in deeply. The tang of salt and peppermint, desert tumbleweed, and the mineral rub of sand. It will be summer in a few months, the hint of its oven-like force already on the breeze, and Annie imagines the long days spent indoors with Lou, the house shut up to the heat, here in this ugly city on the edge of the desert.

She used to live in the mountains, years ago, on the other side of the country. She'd hated it then, or so she told herself, wanting only to escape, but now she looks back on it with longing. At the end of a narrow road, their front door had faced the slope of a hill, the garden designed years earlier by a man of some renown. Lately she has taken to trying to draw it: the dry stone walls, the clusters of tall elegant trees — russet, gold, emerald, and smoke — the thick lush grass that she had to mow until her mother got goats, and the smell of woodfires when the light disappeared behind the ridge.

This time of year brought the first whiff of spring (there was no lurching from bitter winter to the blast of summer), and with it, the crocuses and snowdrops bobbing on delicate green stalks.

Why had she hated it?

She can recall the darkness descending early, the cold steep streets host to late-night drag races, and her own sense that she was not going to meet a man, get married, and have children, that she would forever be an outsider in that country town — but these are just niggling memories of youth and dissatisfaction. Or so she tells herself.

Air so cold and clean it could rip your heart right out, she'd said to Kath recently, who'd glanced up from the brief she was reading to ask her if she'd mind telling Lou her story tonight.

'I'm just swamped.'

'I mind,' Annie had said to herself. Never out loud. 'I really mind. I mind so much it hurts.'

But she'd done it, because that was the deal. Kath earned more, so it made sense for Annie to be the one at home.

In her hand she is still clutching the wattle, the gold dust dulled now, and she turns around to the house.

Perhaps they could go to the tropics, she thinks. She'd lived up north once. In a shack above a beach with sand the colour of mango, and a glittering turquoise ocean that breathed all day and all night. She'd been with a man then, the last man she'd ever been with, and she remembers lying on gritty sheets, looking at the linear planes of his body and wishing something was hidden. Because it never was with him.

Or the snow? If she closes her eyes, she can smell the mud, twigs, and pine, she can hear the crunch as she breaks the crust …

Kath is back. In the kitchen. She has brought supplies for dinner, and she is singing *Lou, Lou, Skip to my Lou*, as she unpacks them.

'Annie?'

She calls her again: 'Annie?'

It's Lou who gives her away, who points to where she stands in the middle of this small patch of lawn, not so difficult to see really, if Kath came out and looked for her, rather than waiting for Annie to go in to Kath.

She raises her hand, somewhat pathetically, and calls out hello, she's just smelling the scent of summer in the air, she'll be in in a minute. She will. But Kath isn't really listening. She simply likes to know where Annie is.

Two hours before dinner, the power goes.

It is the silence that Annie notices first. The hum of the computer, the soft whirr of the fan-forced oven (slow-cooked lamb), and the television all stop. It is only five o'clock, still just enough light to see, but she looks for candles in case it lasts into the evening.

They have four. Horrible scented things in glass jars and floral tins. Unwanted gifts kept in the bottom of the kitchen cupboard. She puts them on the table and then pretends to search for the matches. She knows exactly where they are. Behind the coffee cups and next to the last of a pouch of tobacco she bought two weeks ago and hid in shame. There is no one in the kitchen with her, so she doesn't really need to pretend to look, but she does, even saying 'Ah ha' out loud when she puts her fingers on the box.

'Blackout,' Kath tells her when she comes in from the fuse box. 'The whole street.' She lifts Lou up and sits her on the kitchen table. 'No lights. No TV. Nothin'.'

'For how long?' Lou asks.

'Who knows.'

Two hours later there is still no power. Annie rings the hotline on her mobile every fifteen minutes. She keys in their postcode and the message is always the same. *A power outage has been identified in your area. The cause is [pause] unknown. Power is expected to be returned in [pause] approximately three hours.*

'No news,' she tells Kath every time, finding this pleasing and exciting.

Jane and Sarah arrive with more candles, a torch, and a bottle of wine. The blackout is in their street too — five blocks away.

Jane pours them all a drink, except Sarah, who is pregnant, although they both insist on referring to the pregnancy with the collective noun.

'Cheers,' Jane says. 'Here's to the darkness,' and there is a hardness in her eyes, a darting distance that Annie recognises. Jane will be drunk within the hour.

'I put four dogs down today,' Jane tells them, but Annie is the only one who is listening. Kath is heating the lamb on the gas stove and Sarah is reading a story to Lou. 'I hate Fridays.'

'Maybe you should stop doing it for a while,' Annie says.

Jane rolls her eyes. 'I've asked in staff meetings, it's just a day a week, but they all have excuses — study, kids — and until I can find another volunteer, I'm stuck. I can't leave them in the lurch.' She inhales deeply. 'Lamb?'

Kath holds a wooden spoon out to her and Jane takes the taste. They had been lovers before Annie met Kath. Both tall, lean, handsome women who liked other women — and drinking — too much. The first time Annie briefed Kath at the legal centre, she felt she would burn up from desire. If she shifted just a little, their legs would touch, silky skin on silky skin, and she was daring then, the skim of her calf against Kath's enough to catapult them towards each other, Jane turning up in the middle of the night, drunk, and forcing open the front door, demanding that Kath come out now.

Annie pours herself another drink. The room is dark,

the candles flickering pale. The one closest to her is cloying, chemical in its perfume, and she would like to open the window to the freshness of the night air, but she knows Kath would complain that it's too cold.

Once, years ago, Annie and Jane almost went to bed together. She remembers. The softness of Jane's mouth and the hesitation, the instant when she could have crossed the line. It was Jane who'd stepped back, squeezing Annie's fingers in her own and then letting go. They had never referred to it, and sometimes Annie wonders whether she perhaps imagined the moment. Like the night she packed the car and left — not wanting to have a baby, knowing that and only that, driving just to the edge of the motorway, before coming back again, and bringing her case in, unpacking everything before Kath got home from work. Never mentioned.

In the doorway, Sarah runs her hand over her stomach, and tells them all that Lou has crashed. 'Here's to ours being that easy,' she says. 'Let's hope the Compliant Gene was in donor 107.' She looks at Kath and laughs. 'I don't think it came from you.'

Kath rolls her eyes to the ceiling. 'What do you mean? Look at me, the picture of domesticity after a hard week fighting those mining companies, or at least trying to hold them back a little. Miss Compliant through and through.'

Annie grins. 'Well, it didn't come from me. Nothing came from me.' She is pissed. Lord help her. And saying the wrong thing. Before any of them can leap in and correct her, talk about her hours of care, the time she spends with Lou, she picks up her phone. 'I want to check the emergency line again.'

'Not again.' Kath tries to take the mobile from her. 'It is what it is. A blackout.'

The woman's voice is thin through the speaker: *A power outage has been identified in your area. The cause is [pause] unknown. Power is expected to be returned in [pause] approximately three hours.*

'They know nothing,' Annie says. 'How can they know nothing? In this day and age?' She turns her phone off, not wanting to waste the little battery that is left. 'Maybe there's been a bomb. A terrorist attack. One of the mines?'

'What are you talking about?' Kath just shakes her head. 'The mines are thousands of miles away. They run on their own power.'

'Or a solar flare.' Annie remembers reading about solar flares, years ago, when she read.

Sarah hands the plates around. 'Maybe you just get more anxious now you're a mother.'

'I'm not anxious,' Annie tells her. 'Just curious. Perhaps even excited.'

'About a fucking terrorist attack?' Jane is grinning now. 'Jesus. I thought I was in a bad way.' She pours them both another drink, making certain she doesn't meet Sarah's gaze.

'There was a brief period in which Jane tried to respect the fact that we're pregnant. Cut down on the booze. Go to bed early. Exercise.' Sarah rolls her eyes. 'It was brief.'

'And pointless,' Annie laughs. 'Someone should have a bit of fun.'

Jane raises her glass. The clink is loud. 'I reckon there's more abandoned dogs now than there ever was. People come west to work at the mines and then leave. How could they not take their dog with them? Or at least have the decency to be with them when they're put down?' She stares out at the darkness of the garden. 'There's this moment, this slipping over from life to death, and when you have your hand on an animal as it crosses, it seeps into you. It's the stillness, the dulling of the pupils. They don't close their eyes when they're dead. They're open. And they are just the same. But they are not the same. Not at all.' She puts her glass down. 'I hate Fridays.'

Sarah reaches across the table and puts her hand on Jane's. She shifts her glass away. 'I know you do.'

'We can't even play music,' Annie says. She hums softly to herself, looking at Kath as she does so. 'I used to sing,' she tells the table. 'When I was at law school.'

And she did. She was in a band that played bad angst-ridden electro folk, performing in bars and pubs to a scattered handful of drinkers that never listened.

'Are you offering to entertain us now?' Sarah asks.

Annie grins. 'This is a night for country and western,' she tells them all. 'Mournful, with something of a subdued howl at the end. A longing.' She picks at her lamb, which had to be cooked a little too quickly on the stove. 'Kath's leaving me again next week,' she says. 'Karratha this time.'

Kath rolls her eyes. 'It's only two days. And last time I took you both you hated it.'

It's true. They had stayed in a motel wedged between a construction zone and a drive-in bottle shop, the three of them sharing a single room with an air-conditioning unit that rattled and hummed, a constant drone beneath the banging of doors, the reversing of trucks, and the bored arguments of prostitutes and miners haggling over price. In the morning Lou swam in a small turquoise pool, while Annie sat in a sliver of shade and picked at bacon and eggs, congealed fat sweating on her plate. By ten am it was too hot to be outside any longer, and the room too small. They walked through the shopping centre, killing time with all the other mothers and children, picking at a muffin in Koffee Klub, flicking through racks of clothes to Celine Dion, Annie buying Lou a pack of textas and colouring books in the hope that this would pass the afternoon.

'This is the oldest country in the world,' the taxi driver told her, when she asked him to drive her out of town, into the desert, while Lou slept, locked in the motel room.

Bone-white gums stretched up, smooth and worn, to hard blue sky. Red earth, with sand like silt, and in the distance the flares of the mines, and construction, everywhere construction — roads, houses, motels, new estates with cars the size of trucks, boats the size of villas, and family homes the size of apartment blocks, instant gardens and fake stone walls to mark up territory in the new cul de sacs that could never lead anywhere.

When Lou told Kath she'd been left by herself, Kath was furious. How could Annie have left her alone in the hotel? How could she have been so irresponsible?

Annie had no answer. 'Nothing happened,' she said, lamely.

That night they ate slabs of schnitzel, cheese melted over veal, served with a mountain of chips and a tiny bowl of wilted lettuce, cucumber, and soggy tomato that would have cost a fortune to get here. Lou spilt hers all over their bed. Reception told them there were no spare sheets, the bed could not be made up again until they checked out.

'At $500 a night?' Annie was incensed.

The young boy — a German backpacker — just shrugged his shoulders.

And so they lay on the stained mattress cover, Kath stretched out, beautiful in the pale light from the white moon, her body illuminated by the spotlights at the construction zone, the men working all night and sleeping during days too hot to inhabit.

'You said you never wanted to go back.' Kath clears the plates.

Annie had said that. She dips her fingers in the molten wax, letting it coat her skin and harden in the cool air, smooth, a dull pearl cap covering each nail.

'We can do something together,' Sarah offers. 'While Kath's away.'

Sarah is the only one of the four of them who comes from here. Her family lives in a mansion on the river, a white mock-Georgian building with marble tiles and fountains, green lawns fed by bore water, and a jetty for mooring the boat. Sarah met Jane shortly after Kath ran off with Annie. She came into the vet surgery with her border collie. Four days later, Jane moved in with her.

'She's young, I know,' Jane told them both. 'But I've never been in love like this.'

Kath wisely ignored the remark.

Sarah was a national swimmer. She'd just missed out on a place in the Olympic team after a shoulder injury interrupted her training. She now gave motivational speeches on adversity and triumph, and when she wasn't doing that she shopped, took copious amounts of drugs (until she became pregnant), and stayed out even later than Jane, a feat that initially worried Jane when she came over to visit Kath and Annie, hungover but glowing with the joy of new sex.

It was Sarah who'd wanted a baby, Sarah who'd paid for the IVF and the renovation that gave them a huge family room and a spare bedroom for Sarah's mother, who promised to come and stay and look after her grandchild.

'And try and crack onto Jane,' Annie had laughed. Because Sarah's mother wasn't much older than them and she liked to flirt with the lesbians.

'You can bring Lou over and she can help me set up the baby room.' Sarah had gone over to the couch on the other side of the room and was lying in the darkness, wrapped in a rug. 'We could even have a sleepover.'

Annie stood slowly and walked over to the back door. 'It's so dark out there.' And it was. Not a light for miles. She looked out at the shapes and shadows in their back garden, and she knew she could identify each one. The table, the benches, the pots, the two trees. High overhead, a thin sliver of moon hung in the darkness of the sky, a swirl of stars around it. She remembered camping when she was young, her mother taking her and her sister to 'understand the beauty of the world'. Those were her words. And Annie did understand it. The three of them by the fire, quiet in the immensity of the night, just the hiss and splutter of the flames, and they would try and do as their mother asked, to drink it in, through the skin, all the glory of it filling her small heart, beating and swelling, beating and swelling, both of them swearing to protect the earth, to tread lightly, always and forever. She loved her mother then. A girl who was young and unaware of how eccentric their family was.

She dials the number again: *A power outage has been identified in your area. The cause is [pause] unknown. Power is expected to be returned in [pause] approximately three hours.*

'Maybe this is it,' she tells the others. 'It's all over and we just don't know it yet.'

Later, when they are alone, Kath asks her what's wrong. 'You were in a strange mood.'

They are brushing their teeth by candlelight, in the quiet of their house.

Annie tells her that she is fine, and she kisses Kath as she used to kiss her, all that time ago when they first met, drinking her up, her mouth like mint, cool and sweet on her own.

She sits with Lou for a few moments, watching her sleep in the darkness, the small miracle of that absence from the world, the disappearance of the self that sleep brings, and then she strokes the soft down of her cheek and leaves her.

'I just want to see how far the blackout goes,' she tells Kath, whispering in the quiet.

She is already asleep, and so Annie shuts the door softly behind her and goes out onto their street.

There are no lights for as far as she can see.

In the car she remembers that she forgot to tell Kath about the wattle. She would like that story, the image of Lou waddling making Annie smile.

And then she starts to drive, her phone with so little charge, and her wallet by her side. She will just go as far as the blackout stretches, she tells herself, and on she goes, the lights out in each suburb she enters, only an occasional candle to give any indication of life. Just one more street, she tells herself, promising that she'll then turn for home, but the blackness stretches forever and she keeps on driving.

LAST ONE STANDING

When winter comes, Aisla stays in bed. Outside, shards of ice glint black across the frosted ground. Sometimes the fog rises from the river, thick and damp, resting like a flannel on her mouth and on her lungs. And so she lies there, wrapped in worn blankets, her clothes piled on top for extra warmth, the sound of the dog's raspy breath a comfort in the stillness.

There are days when she doesn't get up until after noon — or at least that is what she supposes the time to be — the sun, when it rises, well above the escarpment on the other side of the river as she collects the water she needs. The pump gave up long ago, and so she carts a bucket down, bringing up icy clear loads, taking care that too much doesn't slosh over the edge, and pouring it into a closed barrel she keeps at the top of the bank. The grass is long now, even the handheld mower no longer useful, the blades too blunt to cut through the stalks, and it slashes her legs until she reaches the steep muddy incline that leads down to the sandy edge.

Sometimes she remembers swimming here as a child, just a brief flash, like an image suddenly appearing on a screen — her and her sister splashing each other, their skin white and dimpled in the cold.

The dog no longer comes with her. She is too old and tired. Instead she waits for her at the top of the path, tail beating a greeting as Aisla makes her way up, breathing heavily with the weight of the bucket. Her coat is greying now, wiry strands beneath Aisla's chilled fingers, the smell of her warm, like old wool, and Aisla buries her face in her neck, breathing her in before turning back to the river.

Five buckets is a good day.

There aren't many good days anymore.

The last load is used to wash herself down, an icy splash across the tautness of her skin, dried out from the cold, metallic and bracing.

Next is the wood.

This is difficult. There is little left close to home, or little that is within easy reach. First she collects whatever has fallen to the ground and then she travels further afield, pushing the wheelbarrow over clumps of dirt, rocks, and ruts. Now that she rarely heats the house, she doesn't need much, just enough to cook an occasional meal and boil water for cleaning — although even that doesn't happen as much as it used to.

The dog comes with her for this chore. She walks slowly, heavy body swaying, legs unsteady, the rhythm to her gait like an irregular heartbeat.

Edna was her name. They called her that because they thought she looked like an old woman, even when she was a puppy.

Once the barrow is full, Aisla wheels it back, her body almost warm now. The dog stops frequently, tottering slightly as she sniffs a clod of dirt, or scratches in the grass. When she barks, Aisla is surprised. It has been so long since she has heard her make a sound.

'Here,' she calls her.

The dog has her nose raised to the sky and is sniffing. She barks again.

It must be an animal.

Food is next. There is a small garden for vegetables, although its output is minimal. Weedy lettuces, bush tomatoes when the weather is warm, potatoes, pumpkins, and squash. Seeds saved and replanted. Aisla also puts out traps. She'd found them at a neighbouring house, jagged mouths of metal ready to clamp shut, and she'd carried them back, jangling in her bag.

I don't eat meat, she used to say. For environmental reasons.

It took a while before she got the hang of baiting them, her first rabbit snared, bloody, and flyblown. Her mouth had watered at the thought of the taste. She'd considered sharing it with the dog, and then she'd changed her mind. In those days the dog was still hunting — disappearing in the night and returning scratched, tired, and content. Now that she was well past her prime and no longer capable, Aisla was scrupulous in dividing up the flesh.

Standing at the edge of the dense scrub, Aisla sniffs the breeze. There is wood burning — the tang of eucalypt, oily and astringent, hovering and then gone.

The dog barks again.

'Shh,' Aisla tells her.

She walks slowly and quietly, her feet scrunching on fallen leaves and twigs, her breath too loud, her heart thudding. Behind her, the dog waits. As she emerges from the poplar grove, she sees it: the remains of a fire, still smoking. Instinctively, she calls the dog to her side — a nod and a click of the fingers. What she lacks in speed, she makes up for in immediate obedience.

Together they stand, looking at the embers in the distance, grey ash.

And then Aisla turns, both of them hurrying back to the house.

It has been so long since she bolted the door. She cannot remember the last time. When she'd first arrived, and there had still been a few others, she had kept it unlocked. They'd all helped each other, traded, taught each other what little they knew that might help them survive.

*She'd grown up with Aaron — had dismissed him as a
dullard who'd stayed in the country, while she'd got a degree,
two, in fact — law and economics. He was the one who'd
taught her to save seeds, to chop wood, to sharpen an axe and
a knife on a whetstone.*

As she tries to slide the bolt now, it won't move.
She pushes it, and then takes the hammer to knock it
through, but misjudges the blow. The bend at one end
makes it impossible to force.

If there is someone there, what can she do? She has no
gun. She has a knife, an axe — yes — but does she have
the capacity to use them? She shakes her head and slides
to the floor, back against the door. The dog lifts herself
slowly, her whole body slumping onto Aisla's lap, her eyes
closed as she rests her head. And her breath is even more
rasping, irregular as her gait.

The next morning Aisla wakes earlier than usual. In fact, she
has slept so fitfully, there seems to be no clear demarcation
between consciousness and unconsciousness. The dog's
chest rattles as she breathes, loud as an engine. She looks
down at her and tells her not to die. *Please. Not yet.*

There is rain this morning — soft grey rain that has
no ebb or flow just a steady constancy, the *drip drip drip*
into all the drums that Aisla has left around, the only
comfort to be found in the bleakness of the day. She will
not have to collect water for a while.

She has a raincoat by the back door. So long unworn, it has gathered dust.

The dog looks at her as she steps out onto the verandah and then goes back into the bedroom. If she called her she would follow, but Aisla lets her be.

Today she would like to warm the house. Her supply of wood is low, and there will be little chance of gathering any dry kindling. She also knows the smoke would make her presence more obvious. Not that she has been hidden. He or she would be bound to know she was here. But to advertise warmth and comfort?

The ground is slippery, oozing mud. She walks slowly and carefully, heading in the same direction as yesterday. Again she smells smoke, but this time it is coming from further upriver, and it hangs more constant in the damp. She ducks her head under branches; wet leaves slap across her skin and her hair is sodden on her neck, dripping down the back of her coat. She passes the Taylor's house, long empty, weeds pressing against each wall, weeds tangled in the doorway, wooden verandah collapsed, one jagged silvery board bolt upright like a slap.

Kissing Mikey Taylor for a dare — running up and pressing her lips against his, only to find he didn't want to let her go.

The gate that marks the end of their land swings open. For so long she used to always shut it behind her. She can't remember how she left it last time she was here. Open, or closed and since opened by another?

Aaron's house is the last before the escarpment. Unlike her family and the Taylors, he'd lived here, walking miles to the bus that took him to school each morning.

His father grew oranges. His mother was dead. He stayed shy on the verandah when their parents had told them to go and ask him to play.

'Can't you talk?' Aisla had once asked him, shitty that she'd had to walk all the way up here, knowing he would simply shake his head or run inside and hide when he saw her approach.

Of course he didn't answer and she'd picked up a pebble, chucking it angrily in the direction of his house, before running all the way back to where her sister and Mikey waited by the river.

She has not been back to his house since she cleaned it out, taking what little food was left, his few tools, clothes and bedding, all in her wheelbarrow. It had been still that day, each footfall echoing against the escarpment, the shriek of a cockatoo loud in the emptiness. The dog had stuck right by her side as she had made that journey home — the two of them the last ones standing.

Now, as she looks down the drive, she sees the smoke coming out of the chimney and her heart lurches, flying and falling, at the sight. Oh god, how she wishes the dog were here with her. The dog would know what to do, and she shakes her head at the foolishness of the thought.

And so she stands, paralysed, the rain sluicing down, all of her sodden, knowing she will need fire to dry her clothes, warmth when she gets home. She could go there, she thinks, knock on that door and see who opens it, welcome them to this place that she used to love without ever even knowing that she loved it. Because that was the way it was.

But she doesn't.

She just stands there in the rain until her shoes are full and she is so cold she can no longer feel her fingers, the skin white and wrinkled, bloodless, and then she turns for home.

The dog does not move when she opens the door. She is always waiting when Aisla returns, tail wagging, mouth open in a yellow-toothed grin. Aisla clicks her fingers. Nothing. She calls for her, a trail of water soaking into the floorboards as she heads straight to her bedroom.

And there she is, lying on the floor next to the unmade bed, glancing up at Aisla but unable to wag her tail, to thump it even.

You cannot die.

She brings a bowl of water to her, scooping a handful and taking it straight to the dog's mouth. Her tongue is dry as she laps at it, and then lets her head sink back to the floor.

She will light a fire. A big fire like she used to light.

She builds it carefully, using the last of the dried kindling and bringing in two of the largest stumps of wood — wood she has been saving, although she is no longer sure what for. She has rabbit too, and she will carve off some for the dog and cook the rest for herself.

But the dog won't eat.

She licks at the bone and then puts her head down, closing her eyes.

Aisla tries to coax her, holding out small morsels, whispering to her that it tastes delicious. 'Mmmm,' she says like a blabbering idiot. 'Mmmm.'

She puts it back in a bowl and covers it.

Lowering herself to the floor, she rests the dog's head in her lap.

And outside, the rain continues.

The next morning, Aisla wakes to silence. It is the absence of rain she notices first. All night it had drummed on the roof, steady, constant, soothing.

Hammering tin around the chimney, Aaron had told her it would hold for years. You'd be surprised, he'd said, at how long things last.

And then she realises the dog is not lying by her bed. The rasp of that breath, the wheezing rattle has been her companion for so long that she no longer heard it — but its absence was loud.

She looks down to where the dog always lies, bracing herself for what she does not want to see. The worn carpet is bare, just whirls of her hair, clumps of it, white like an old woman's.

After Aaron had gone, Aisla had tried to get the dog to lie on the bed with her. She wanted warmth. The dog was appalled — jumping up only because she'd been told to, slinking off as soon as a respectable amount of time had passed.

Aisla's breath comes in puffs of white frost, and she wraps her coat close as she looks through the house. There is nothing. Just the remains of last night's fire and the small covered bowl with the rabbit in it. The front door is ajar, cold air slicing through the room. She calls the dog tentatively, but stops almost as soon as she starts, suddenly afraid.

It is a child.

She is thin, malnourished.

She sits on the edge of the verandah, sniffling, one dirty hand trailing through the dog's coat.

'Who are you?' Aisla asks, startled by the sound of her own voice forming a sentence.

'Mary,' the child tells her, rubbing the back of her hand across her eyes.

'Are you alone?'

The child nods.

'How'd you get here?'

'Walked.'

'Where from?'

The child points in the direction of Aaron's house.

'Before that?'

She points the other way.

'Where are your parents?'

She looks down at the verandah. 'Is your dog sick?'

The dog hasn't moved from the child's side.

Aisla bends down and strokes the top of her head. 'She's old.'

'Is she dying?'

Aisla nods.

It is enough to make her sink to the ground, back against the wall of the house, knees to her chest. Staring up at the soft grey of the sky, she says nothing.

I don't want to be the last one, she'd whispered. Past hearing, Aaron had not comforted her. No one could comfort her. But the dog. She had put her head in Aisla's lap and together they had kept watch.

'Do you have food?' the child asks. She has a bag by her side and she pushes it towards Aisla. Inside are two tins — one of tomatoes, one of spaghetti.

'My grandma saved them for me. These are the last ones.'

'Are you hungry?' Aisla asks, her own mouth salivating at the thought of something other than potato or rabbit.

The child nods.

She does not know if she still has a can opener. It's been so long. She searches in the drawers, utensils clattering. She cannot even remember the last time she used a knife or fork, she thinks. Just her and the dog. Gnawing on whatever they could scrounge up.

As she finds one, the child calls out to her. 'Hey,' she

says. Then: 'Miss,' just as they used to say in school, her voice sharp in the quiet.

The child moves to one side, carefully lifting the dog's head off her lap and placing it on Aisla's.

'She's going,' she whispers.

And it is true. It is horribly true. Each breath is laboured, slow and deep. The dog's eyes are glazed, already empty, fixed on Aisla but not on her, on another place.

Please don't.

She shifts, one paw up on Aisla's leg. Aisla strokes it gently, running her finger along the underside where the fur grows in two directions, meeting in a perfect ridge in the middle. The dog's nails are long, dull black, the pads on her feet shaped like teardrops, calloused to the touch. Her mouth hangs slightly open, saliva gathered on her gums, her teeth worn down and yellowed.

And so Aisla just holds her.

She holds her until there is no longer an intake of breath, until the weight of her body changes, and still she holds her, all of her unwilling, unable, to let her go.

The girl has a bowl of food in each hand. She puts one down next to Aisla and then she reaches out, and runs her finger along the dog's muzzle.

'She's gone?'

Aisla nods.

Sitting cross-legged on the verandah next to her, the girl begins to eat, her head bent low over her bowl. She doesn't speak until she finishes, a red stain around her mouth, a strand of spaghetti on the front of her shirt. She wipes her face with the back of her hand.

'You can't close their eyes when they die,' she says. 'My gran told me that.'

It's true.

Milky and glass-like, the dog's eyes are open.

Pushing the other bowl towards Aisla, the girl tells her to eat.

'You'll need it,' she says.

Her gaze is fixed out towards the row of poplars.

'That looks like as good a spot as any,' the girl says. And then she stands up and goes to get the shovel, her small body stronger than it looks as she carries it over to where the trees stretch, bare branched and slender, and she proceeds to dig. Just like someone who has done this before.

SHIP TO SHORE

Luisa didn't see the house before she agreed to take it. She saw pictures on the internet, but in truth she barely glanced at them. She had simply put in a search for the location, and when she was asked if she wished to refine her criteria, her hand had hovered momentarily over the keyboard. One bedroom or three? It didn't matter. Price? She couldn't imagine there would be much difference between the few shacks that were available for permanent rental.

There were only two. Each with faded paint, blistered woodwork, and curtained windows. When she rang the agent, only one was left. The owner had sold the other one, he said.

'It's fairly primitive,' he added.

That didn't matter, she replied. Could she take it immediately?

He sounded surprised and then quickly told her it was a bargain. 'Places like this rent in holiday season for a couple of thousand a week.'

Luisa told Sam she was going that afternoon. They had each been living their lives as they had always lived them, although his pretence was perhaps a little less rigid than hers. In the last few weeks, he had stopped going into work, often sitting up and drinking on his own until he fell asleep on the couch, his snores loud in the morning, the room dank and stale with sadness. She would look at him lying there, and occasionally she would stroke the lank fall of his hair from his clammy skin, a gesture of tenderness that she could not make when he was awake. Neither of them could; the fear of what it could open was too much.

She had loved him. She probably still did. But all of that was so puny and frail, like an insignificant life form seen from far away, nothing in the face of the raging, roiling force of her grief.

She told him her plans and he nodded.

'You don't need to sell the house. You don't need to change anything. And if you need me —'

He put his hand on hers and told her he understood.

That night they made love for the first time since Marcus' funeral. There was a solicitousness to their physical farewell, as though each could bruise, and afterwards they lay in silence, back to back, the quiet so complete that Luisa could hear a moth fluttering in the kitchen at the other end of the house.

* * *

The agent had told her the place was furnished, but she was, of course, welcome to bring anything of her own.

'There's plenty of storage.' He waved in the direction of the double garage at the other end of the bare lawns.

She bent down and touched the grass, stiff and green, like plastic. The town was not yet on sewerage and received plenty of rainfall; the lawn couldn't help but grow despite the salt of a constant brisk breeze.

There was only one other permanent resident on the street, Connie, whose house was two doors up.

'We're all old here,' she said. 'Apart from Leanne, who does the cleaning, and Gerry, who mows the lawns. But he's pushing sixty. And then there's Terry, the plumber, and Denise, his wife. And all their kids. They're like Summer Bay. All blonde and tanned.' Connie laughed until she coughed, hacking and harsh. She'd been a smoker, years ago. 'Worst thing I ever did.'

Connie had a Jack Russell terrier that barked each time Luisa walked past, a ferocious yap as she ran out onto the road, coming within a metre of Luisa and then darting back inside. Pixie was her name.

She also had a cat — Ginger — who hissed at her, back arched, one torn ear flicking from side to side.

At first, Luisa thought she wouldn't make many changes, but within a week of fresh sea air and abrasive blue winter skies, she found it hard to return to the dimness of those rooms. The nylon netting curtains were yellowed and torn, the divan in the lounge room had cigarette burns, and the beds smelt of urine.

She paid Leanne to help her clean.

They carried everything to the garage and washed the walls and floors, the smell of eucalypt sharp.

Leanne didn't ask questions.

She told Luisa the house had belonged to an old bloke, Jack, who used to fish. 'Died in his bed and wasn't found for a week.' She wrinkled her nose. 'He owned this and the place next door. Kids sold the other one for half a million. Seems wrong them getting all that money when they never even came to see him.'

Luisa ordered new furniture on the internet — generic, cheap, clean, and unlikely to last. It looked like a house in a catalogue, she thought, and she didn't care. It had simply been a matter of removing the smell, the vestiges of Jack that had remained — it had not been a question of adding any sense of herself. That thought was impossible to comprehend.

It was strange how easily her days were filled. Each morning she walked along the main beach. Pixie followed, yapping for the first few metres, and then she just trotted behind, her collar jingling like sleigh bells. The constancy of the sea, sand, and sky were comforting, as was the gradual nature of change. One day the inlet would have deepened, cutting the beach in two. Another, bluebottles would have washed in, and pufferfish, scaly and monstrous on the shore. The next, all would be flat and benign. Large changes, really, but against the enormity of that backdrop, all was small.

Occasionally she would see Gus and Dave, who went out to fish. They would nod — nothing more. Some mornings, weekenders would be down, trim and neat in their jogging gear, running their dogs up the beach. They were often more eager to talk, to comment on the weather or a change in town.

After her walk she went to the shop and bought the paper. Soon she began to pick one up for Connie as well. She talked to Bev briefly, news of an accident, or a cold front coming in, as she handed over her $2 coins.

It was strange reading the *Herald* as she looked out at her bare stretch of lawn, framed by a rusted tin fence and the double garage, which was now filled with Jack's old furniture. Occasionally an article would remind her of someone she once knew, her friend Alison, who worked for Greenpeace, or David, who was a Consumer Rights Activist, or Liesel, who loved netball and was furious at how little media attention it received. They would be talking about this, she would think, over dinner or breakfast, somewhere in that planet far away where they all still lived.

They rang her sometimes, these friends. When she was foolish enough to answer the phone without thinking, they would suggest coming to visit, or perhaps her returning to town for the weekend.

'Sure,' she would say. 'But not yet. I just need to be left alone for a while.'

And soon the calls stopped.

During the day there were enough chores to slowly fill the hours. She could drive into Nowra to buy food. There was washing to be done. Weeds to be pulled up. Even windows that could be cleaned. And then there was the afternoon walk, as the sky purpled over the ocean and Pixie trotted behind her, collar jingling.

Another day was done.

The first time she heard the explosion, Luisa thought the house might fold, wall by wall, collapsing in on itself. A deep thudding boom shook the floors, the cheap crockery on the shelves rattled, the cutlery in the drawer shook, metal on metal, and then a brief still, until the second thud, louder than the first, made the windows also shudder, adding to the chorus of complaint. It reminded her of a time years ago, on that other planet, when she and Sam had travelled to Portugal, the place where Marcus was conceived. They woke to find the whole town on the beach, the old women with their skirts pulled over their heads, everyone gathered for the spectacle of a building being imploded — gone to make way for the building of a new hotel.

But here there is nothing, and no one.

She stands out on the road, waiting to see if Connie

will come out, or anyone really, to tell her that the world is coming to an end. This is it. Thank Christ.

High in the bleached branches of gum tree, four kookaburras swoop down and laugh. That's it. The only sound.

And then the boom happens again, louder this time, and she goes straight to Connie's door.

What's happening? she wants to ask, but Connie's complete lack of concern silences the question before it's uttered.

A fourth boom, and Luisa grips the doorframe and looks at Connie in a panic.

Connie's laugh soon descends into her usual hacking cough. When she finally stops, she opens the door a little wider to ask Luisa in.

'Ship to shore,' she tells her. She hands her a cup of weak, sugary tea, and Luisa takes it, pushing Pixie to one side as the dog tries to leap into her lap.

'The naval base,' Connie continues, seeming surprised by Luisa's lack of awareness of their neighbours.

Luisa nods — she has seen the signs at the entrance of the town — and she has heard about the beaches on the bay when the base is open to the public.

'They do practice explosions, take the ships out in the winter months. You can walk out to the headland and see 'em if you want.'

* * *

Two days later she follows the track out through the bush, Pixie trotting along behind her. The map at the shelter isn't much help — it just shows a confusing maze of dotted lines — but she figures that keeping the sea to her left and heading up the rise will take her to the cliff edge.

The bush is dense; tangled bony twigs of knotted dry banksia, sprays of crimson woollsia, and burnt orange bottlebrush like candelabra press close on either side. Great tracts are muddy puddles, tea-tree brown and murky, and Pixie stops to drink at each one, her tongue lapping the surface of the water before she trots ahead, darting into each burrow of scrub, fast on the scent of rabbit or wallaby.

Luisa calls her over and over, wishing she hadn't followed, because to lose her would be too awful; to have to tell Connie that Pixie was out there somewhere, alone and unable to find her way home, is too much to countenance.

It takes ten minutes for Pixie to emerge, panting and scratched. Luisa could hear her barking in the bush, tangled up and unable to escape. She tries to pick the dog up, but Pixie squirms out of her grasp and is gone again.

The whole peninsula is sandstone, and the path soon fades into bleached silica littered with dried tea-tree leaves. On her left Luisa can see the horizon, steely sea against steely sky. Pixie, who suddenly emerges from the scrub once more, runs ahead again, and Luisa lets her go, realising there is little point in calling her back.

The edge of the cliff is sudden, and out there on the metallic sea are the gunships, grey as the ocean; at her feet is the drop, horrifying in all the possibility it holds, her stomach sickening as she contemplates the descent.

Luisa had been the one with Marcus when the seizure had come. Normally, if she could get a valium into him, she could stop it, but this time she had been too late. He had stopped breathing.

He was only four years old.

Sometimes late at night, her phone rings. She sees Sam's name on the screen and she picks it up. Neither of them speak. She just lies there, and so does he, both of them silent, their breath the only connection, seemingly frail, but so vital that its strength cannot be readily dismissed.

At her feet, Pixie darts out again, and she bends to catch her, unaware that she is crying until she realises that she cannot see, the salt of her tears and the salt of the wind blurring her vision, and Pixie squeals as Luisa treads on her paw, losing her grip on her tail, and then she is gone, scrambling sideways over the cliff, yelping as she lands on a small outcrop, too far for Luisa to reach.

The boom is sonic, deep, and overwhelming as they send another from ship to shore, and Luisa leans over the edge, telling Pixie to *stay*, be still, *stay*.

Oh God, she thinks as she runs back along the path, *oh, God, please don't let them send another one in, please don't let her fall*, and she splashes back through the puddles, twigs slashing across her arms and face, until she reaches the town, not sure who to ask or what to do in this strange place of old people where she is all alone and trying to save a dog she has never even liked.

It is Gus who comes back out with her. He is in the shop, his catch of the day delivered. He has a rope and a basket. 'And bait,' he adds, taking a styrofoam tray of mince from the fridge.

'She doesn't do as she's told,' Luisa tries to explain to him.

He grunts and looks at her, eyes red rimmed, face unshaven, broad fingers smelling of fish guts as he rubs his palm across his chin. 'Well, she'd better learn fast.'

Luisa cannot bring herself to look over the edge, but Gus lies on his stomach and faces down to where the sea crashes far below.

'Still there,' he tells her. He holds a finger to his lips signalling the need for quiet.

Luisa lies next to him. Pixie is curled up into a ball, her body shaking.

Out in the ocean, the ships wait.

'Will they send another one in?' Luisa whispers.

Gus doesn't respond. He is tying the rope through the basket weave, trying to stabilise it with a web underneath. There is barely room on the ledge for Pixie, let alone the basket as well.

'When I lower it, call her. Not excited. Just soft.'

Later, when Luisa remembers it all, she realises that her awareness of the plummet, the possibility of the drop, is gone as she leans right over that cliff, looking down to where ocean crashes and heaves and sighs.

She just calls Pixie's name, hoping her voice is carrying above the sough of the wind — not too much, but enough to be reassuring. 'Pixie,' she says. 'Pixie.' And Pixie looks up to where the basket hovers, half on the ledge, half hanging in the air, the mince inside, just out of her reach.

'In you go,' Luisa urges.

Her nose is in the air, twitching, her tail wagging, hesitant.

Luisa glances out to the ships. They are still, hulking metal, like crouching beasts.

Oh God, Luisa thinks again as Pixie stands slowly, her nose in the basket.

Next to her Gus shifts the ropes so that the basket lowers, the top level with the outcrop. He has to hold it steady now. Not a movement, not until Pixie is in there.

She inches closer, careful in the stiffness of the breeze, and she drops her nose in. Almost there.

'Good girl,' Luisa tells her. 'Good girl.'

And then she does it, with all the delicate balance of a dog, the beauty of that half-leap, half-step too much for Luisa to bear, as the boom resounds, right through her core, ripping her asunder, eyes closed to the full force of it, the shattering of self as the ships send another to shore, oblivious to Gus carefully raising the basket, and Luisa lying next to him, holding onto the cliff edge, fingers white on sandstone, eyes closed as the force rips through her once again.

'Got her,' Gus says.

And Luisa sits up slowly. 'Keep her in the basket,' she tells him. 'Just keep her in the basket.'

That night, when the phone rings, and Sam's name is there on the screen, Luisa speaks.

'Ship to shore?' she whispers to him. 'Ship to shore?'

And his reply, when it comes, is as quiet as her question. 'Shore to ship,' he says, and nothing more.

STILL BREATHING

That summer, I was diagnosed with glandular fever. Each night the sweats came, as oppressive as the long days in that small town, and as I lay on top of crumpled sheets, I lurched from dream to dream, waking too tired to get up.

I was in a share house in the centre of the city, and my room had no windows. The cell, we called it, when we first signed the lease, and its lack of light or ventilation meant I paid a little less than Rachel.

We were students. She was studying medicine, and I was about to start the final year of a fine arts degree, majoring in photography, with plans to move east as soon as I finished.

I often didn't rise until the afternoon light turned the hallway a deep gold, and I would shuffle out to the lounge room, where Rachel would be lying on the art deco couch, oblivious to how ill I felt. We were young, and didn't realise that sharing a house could also entail caring for each other — which was not as harsh as it sounds. Neither of us had expectations of the other, and so there was little sense of being let down. But in that month of fever, I sometimes wished I had a home to go to.

On the days when I tried to wash my bedding clean of the night sweats, I would be exhausted by the time I brought it all in from the line, unable to actually put sheets on the bed until I had slept again. A couple of times I asked Rachel to help, and she did, but not in the calm, efficient way I longed for. Sitting on my mattress, cigarette in her hand, she would talk about herself. She had been in love with a man called Simon for as long as I had known her, and she obsessed over him. Perhaps he had talked to her the previous evening and she needed to tell me every word he had said, or maybe she had seen him with another woman and wanted to know whether she was his girlfriend, or he might have told her he was going to see a band that was coming to town, was it an invitation for her to join him? At that particular point in time, it was his visits that she analysed — was he really coming to bring me meals or was it just an excuse to spend time with her?

She didn't actually want my opinion — which was fortunate, as the little interest I had once had in the topic had gone even before the onset of the virus — she just enjoyed weaving a soap opera without end as she forgot to smoke, and the ash from her cigarette crumpled to the floor, and my bed remained unmade.

Rachel's obsession with Simon didn't stop her from sleeping with other men, but she chose men who were just passing through, guitarists or singers in bands that came to town for a couple of nights and played at one of the two local clubs.

Rachel was tall and striking — she had shaved her bleached blonde hair close to her head, and she had eyes like a cat's, amber and still, fringed by heavy mascara and kohl, her lips painted a deep red. She wore clothes from op shops, beautiful beaded cocktail dresses or fifties cropped pants and checked shirts knotted at the waist. I had never known her to pay for entry to either of the two clubs in that town — the doormen knew her, always calling her to the front of the queue with a quick nod.

She would dance all night, often not needing to introduce herself to the band at the end of their set. Once they had finished playing, they came and drank at the bar, one of them sidling up to Rachel, buying her a drink, lighting her cigarette, and asking her what she did.

'I'm studying to be a doctor,' she would tell them, enjoying their surprise as they reassessed her. 'Two years to go. Unless I specialise.'

When she returned home, her pale skin scrubbed of make-up, eyes black apart from a smudge of kohl, lips cracked and dry, she'd lie back on the couch and tell me what he was like.

Tragic.

So pissed he couldn't get it up.

Kind of sad. She'd look at me and roll her eyes. These were the ones that wanted to see her again the next evening, who told her they were homesick and missed their girlfriends or children.

It was rare that she would speak of them in favourable terms, and if she did it was usually only in reference to their body.

Sometimes she left them when they were still asleep. Once or twice she had even taken money from them.

His wallet was there, she would say. *He'd spent the entire night telling me how miserable he was. I might as well be paid.*

Even though we often went to the club together, and there was always more than one band member wanting sex or comfort, I never went home with one of them. By the time the gig was finished and she was at the bar, I would either have gone back to our place or on to someone's house, or perhaps to eat souvlaki at the one late-night takeaway place, frequented by taxi drivers and the stoned or drunk. I didn't know how to talk to people I did not know, and the thought of going to a hotel, alone with a stranger, only held fear for me. In any event, I would have been the second prize, the one that the drummer picked up, or the roadie.

I knew Simon, Rachel's obsession, from art school. He was quiet and shy, his canvases monochromatic, the exact hue a matter of great importance to him. The bitumen at sunset, the muddy brown of a puddle at the edge of the parklands, the batter on a piece of fish — he knew exactly what it was he wanted.

He lived three streets away, and when we saw each other at school or near home, we would talk. I never mentioned Rachel and nor did he. Our talk was of books we loved, or a piece of music, or our latest work. Sometimes he made me mixed tapes, but he didn't give them to me as gifts of love, it was just a desire to share the rush of joy at creative perfection. He loved The Smiths and The Cure, and he drove a vintage Rover, a beautiful car with a walnut dash. He had an old taxi sign that he put on the roof, and he used it when there was a rare influx of visitors to that town for a special event — the Grand Prix or the cricket.

In the couple of months before I became ill, I had got to know Simon a little better when I started a tentative relationship with Nate, his flatmate. At twenty-five, Nate was older than us. He worked as a waiter at night and had been writing a novel for years. At first I listened when he told me what it was about; sometimes he read me short segments while we lay in bed together, the night too hot for our bodies to remain close. The central character was in a coma, able to hear the thoughts of his family and friends who gathered around his bedside, but unable to utter a word himself.

Nate wrote well, and I didn't mind listening. The

problem was that he didn't know how to create an entire tale around his idea, and so it had stayed poised, stuck in the middle, sagging with the weight of each polish he gave in place of progress.

Our relationship was hovering at the edge of either drifting apart or slowly revealing a little more of ourselves to each other, when I became ill. We had been down the coast together, spending a day at Willunga, swimming in clear turquoise water and sheltering from the heat in the pink limestone caves, when I knew that I was sick. Shivering and slick with sweat, I told him I needed to go home, but I wasn't sure if I would make it up the long chalky path that wound through the cliffs, harsh white under the hard blue sky. He walked me slowly up that hill and drove me home, his hand too hot on my knee as he tried to offer solicitude while I shivered, teeth chattering, until we reached my house.

I did not even remember him undressing me and putting me into bed, but he must have, with gentleness no doubt — he was a man who could be accused of too frequently proffering a bland, cottonwool kindness — and then he left.

Four days later, when I told him I had been diagnosed with glandular fever, he stepped back a little further, until he was speaking to me from outside the door of my windowless room, his voice nervous as he said he'd better keep away.

'It's contagious, isn't it?'

I was too tired to care if he was there or not, and so I just nodded, the heat of tears in the corner of my eyes, stinging and sharp.

'It's okay,' I said. 'It's just the illness. It's not you.' I realised we seemed to have lurched into something that resembled a break-up conversation and I wasn't quite sure how we had managed to get there or what I felt. I could smell his sweat beneath his tight jeans, and I could see the stains under the armpits of his T-shirt. He was scratching at the long dark hairs on his arms as he backed right into the wall.

'I've just gotta finish the book — and I can't afford to miss any shifts.'

It was fine, I said again, just wanting him gone so I could sleep.

Two nights later I woke to find Simon at the door to my room. He had a meal, he told me, his voice soft and cool in the dark. It was from Nate as well, he added, but I had tasted Nate's two dishes (chops, salad, baked potato, and pasta with tuna and tomato), and I knew. I sat up, not sure if I was imagining the bowl he put in front of me. A stir-fry, he said, and I ate a mouthful, slowly, not because I was hungry but because the kindness was so beautiful, I wanted to show my appreciation.

He came again, every few days, always with something — soup or fruit or bread. He would refill a jug with fresh water and put it by my bed before sitting on the floor at the edge of my room and talking to me for a little while

— unless Rachel was there, in which case she would call him out to the lounge, and he would shrug shyly, telling me he'd say goodbye before he left.

I find it hard to remember our conversations. I was feverish, and the truth and dreams blurred, but I have a recollection of him telling me he had grown up in a cult. He looked embarrassed then, backtracking as soon as he said the word.

'Well that's what other people called it, but they didn't. We didn't. Amazon Acres was the name. All women. I had to leave before I reached puberty.'

'Where'd you go?' I asked, trying to sit myself up a little so that I could see him more clearly, there, leaning against the wall, his olive skin lit by the honeyed afternoon sunlight, his dark eyes gold-flecked, his long slender hands crossed around his knees, which he hugged to his chest. He was beautiful, I realised, but it wasn't a realisation of attraction. Simon was gay. I suppose I had always known what Rachel had failed to see, or maybe she did see it and had picked him as an object of adoration because he was unattainable. Who knows? It wasn't how we thought of the world then — layers of complex analysing were to come later, in our thirties. Not in our twenties.

'One of my mothers, Jacqui, left with me. We lived together until I turned sixteen. She told me as soon as I could beat her in an arm wrestle, I was ready to be on my own. She's in the hills now, on a farm with women only.'

She was the one who had taught him to cook, to care for himself and for others. She had also taught him to play the bass guitar, and to knit. *A strange combination of skills*, he said, his grin shy in the half-dark.

In those weeks of fever, Rachel came and went, the sound of her key in the lock and her heels loud in the hall, letting me know whether she was home or not. Sometimes she put her head around my door to tell me I looked terrible, or to relay a story from the night before.

Gradually I became well enough to get up for short periods, and I would come out of my room when I heard her, or when Simon visited, craving light and human interaction. I felt like a prisoner who'd been locked in the dark, I told her once, and she just looked at me, perplexed.

'You don't have to stay in your room,' she said, oblivious to how weak I'd been.

She was excited. The Droids were playing at the Toucan that weekend. It was a secret gig to try out some of their new songs. Frank the doorman had told her.

'Come with me,' she urged, passing me the joint she'd just rolled.

I waved it away.

'Maybe you should try acupuncture.' She assessed me for a moment, those beautiful eyes narrowed as she took my measure. She was into Chinese medicine that year.

She'd done a short course in herbs, and used the little knowledge she had to question and criticise lecturers. 'Get your immune system strong again. You think Simon would come with me?'

I shrugged. 'Ask him.'

She didn't, of course. When the night came, she went on her own — shimmering in a silver sequinned top and black Thai-silk cropped pants. As she twirled in the entrance to my room, I applauded her beauty, and she curtsied, grinding her teeth slightly as she told me not to wait up.

'Couldn't get any speed,' she explained and she held up an empty packet of diet pills. 'Beggars can't be choosers.' And then she blew me a kiss. 'Why don't you get Nate over?' Her moment of sympathy for my plight passed as I started to tell her I hadn't seen him for some weeks.

'I'll bring you back a Droid,' she laughed, and she was gone.

I woke, not sure if it was night or day, the darkness of my room so permanent time could slide with no markers. I could hear her laughter, and beneath it the sound of a man's voice, rusted and deep. The singer, no doubt. That was who she usually chose. I wondered why they hadn't gone to his hotel, and then I drifted back to sleep, perhaps only briefly, my room still in darkness when I woke again, this time to hear him on the phone.

'Jesus, babe.' Two words he kept repeating. 'I'm on the first flight home.'

I listened as he called out to Rachel, wanting our number, telling the person on the phone he was at a friend's, he hadn't wanted to stay at the hotel. Yep, the flight was at midday, *cross your legs*, he said — and I thought it was the fever then, but my forehead was cool — *love you*, he said, and then there was a loud whoop, followed by what sounded like a tap dance: *Havin' your baby, what a beautiful way* …, the crack in his voice wide enough to drive a truck through as he forgot the words and hooted.

'Dave,' he told me, holding out his hand as I stood at the entrance to the lounge. 'Dad Dave. Not Dad and Dave. Dad Dave. *Havin' your baby …*'

The morning light through the window was pale, the pink of dawn soft and hesitant. I looked at the clock we'd hung on the wall when we first moved in. Six am.

He folded me in his arms, reeking of alcohol and sex. He had no pants on, and I stepped back, glancing down at his penis.

Crossing his legs and cupping himself with his hands, he grinned, beautiful white teeth and crazy blue eyes. 'Apologies.' He bowed. 'I was on my way to visit the facilities when I stopped by the phone to check in with home.'

Rachel was up now, eyes bleary, looking at both of us.

'He's having a baby,' I told her, shrugging.

She glanced at him, eyes running up and down his body, as she shook her head. 'Four years of medical school, and I still didn't know you were up the duff.'

His laughter, when it came, because everything felt strangely delayed, was a loud snort, a chortle, and then he took Rachel in his arms and kissed her on the lips, before dancing her out into the hall.

About an hour later, I heard them having sex. Or rather, I heard him, and I got up then, thinking that maybe I could shower and dress and try and get out of the house for the first time in weeks. Not that I was really strong enough, I just didn't want to listen to the fucked-up mess that was a man having sex with another woman while his girlfriend or wife was giving birth to his baby. That was the truth of it.

The streets were empty, blanketed by a Sunday morning quiet, and I walked slowly, limbs unsteady, the smell of sky and trees overwhelming after weeks inside.

It was Nate who answered the door, wearing the T-shirt he always wore to bed and a threadbare towel tucked around his waist.

Simon wasn't in, he told me, shifting awkwardly from foot to foot.

I knew he had someone in his room and I wanted to tell him it was fine, I wasn't upset, but I was too tired.

I asked if I could just sit for a moment. He didn't have to stay with me, I assured him. But he felt nervous about leaving me alone, or guilty — I didn't know — and our conversation was awkward.

He would tell Simon I had called, he promised as he

waved goodbye. He was glad I was on the mend.

Outside the markets, a few café owners were bringing out tables and putting up umbrellas to provide some relief from the heat that would soon descend. The tables would remain empty for most of the day. This was not a town where people went out on a Sunday, and most places remained closed, the streets empty, church bells ringing in the distance, a few cars slowly cruising the quiet, hot streets.

Like many of my age, I couldn't wait to leave. Cheap rent, op shops that weren't always picked over, the markets, and the ease with which you could gain some notoriety in a place so small were not enough to keep us here. As soon as I finished my studies, I would move to Sydney or Melbourne, I would find work, my life would begin. I had always known this, but on that hot Sunday morning, as I walked slowly back home, wishing I had somewhere else to go, it was as though I had already left. I was floating above the strange emptiness of my past, looking down on myself — my hopes and desires and plans all unsullied, the self that I was to become beckoning, waiting.

I photographed Dave ten years after that morning. I remembered him, but he, of course, had no recollection of who I was. It was a profile piece, to be published in a magazine that has since gone out of business but was, for a brief period, both fashionable and interesting.

We spent a day with him and his family — Daria asking questions, me taking photographs. He talked about surviving in the music industry, the fickleness of success, and the constant nagging desire to write a better song than the last.

Still handsome, he sat outside in the back garden of his Clovelly house, a cattle dog lying in the sun at his feet, and shaded his pale blue eyes from the brilliance of the sky.

'I did a lot of wild things when I was young,' he told Daria. 'I don't regret, but I sometimes look back and ...' His feet tapped against the stone flagging and he rolled himself another cigarette. 'Last vice left.' He grinned sheepishly as he held it up, and I took a photo — the one that was eventually used on the cover. He flicked a fleck of tobacco off his knee. 'But it's what you do. You fuck up.' He scratched the dog's ears and it looked up at him, eyes narrowed in the sunlight. 'And then you reach that dividing line, and you hope you're one of the lucky ones that learns, or is fortunate enough to have someone drag you over.' He looked over to the house, where his partner, Bec, and their four-year-old son, Max, had just returned from the park.

Daria asked him whether he was referring to becoming a parent. 'A lot of people say you don't really grow up until you have a child of your own.'

But he didn't answer, as Max had run out of the house

and grabbed his leg. 'We got pies,' Max said, and his face was smeared with sauce, pastry clinging to the corners of his mouth. Dave lifted him up and I took their photo together.

'I'll send you some of these if you like.'

He looked across at me, some of the sauce now on his cheek, and he asked me when my baby was due.

'Two months,' I said.

'You nervous?' His mouth was crooked as he smiled, eyes still squinting. He had dropped his cigarette to the ground as soon as Max came out, and he picked it up now, flicking it into a rosemary bush. 'I pretend I don't smoke when he's around,' he confessed.

I nodded in response to his question, although he wasn't really interested in an answer.

I'd been pregnant before — twice, in fact. Miscarrying at four months the first time and at six months the second time. Every day I woke, terrified of losing this baby, the fear like a corrosive current. Not that anyone would have known. I didn't speak of it.

From inside the house, Bec called out to us. Lunch was ready.

'You going to join us?' he asked.

I wondered whether Bec had been the mother of that first child ten years ago, the one he'd lost, or whether she was part of his new life, here on this side of the line. And as I looked at him, there in the bright morning light, I remembered returning home that morning ten years ago, to find him in the hallway of the house I shared with Rachel, knees clutched to his chest, the phone by his side. I could smell the sourness of vomit, and there was, in his eyes, the strange distance that descends after panic. I don't think he even knew who I was as I opened our front door, the light from the street spilling in, already white in its heat, and he flinched.

Rachel came out then, her keys in her hand, her face also pale.

'The baby didn't breathe,' she whispered to me.

I'd had no idea what to say to him, a man I didn't know, and so I had leant down, slightly hazy from the strangeness of having left the house after months, and I took his hand. 'You need to get home,' I said, and I'd helped him up, leading him to where Rachel waited, keys in hand.

As I began to pack up my camera gear, the memory of that morning brought with it the ghost of my youth, and I could see myself as I was ten years ago, wanting to be grown up, gone from that place for good, so sure that the next place would be better.

It is strange how often we long for life to move forward; *I just have to get through this*, we think, as though the past, with all its fears and fuck-ups and anxieties, can be completely left behind, neat, contained, never spilling over the line we imagine is waiting for us. And yet the past is always there, hovering at the edge, teasing us, reappearing when we least expect it, and then sliding away again, where it waits, the warmth of its breath reminding us that it still lives.

SUNDAY

Every day, Hannah called home from the office. She usually waited until about the third flat spot in the morning, and then she quickly dialled.

The answering machine message hadn't been changed for years: *You've called Hannah and Jeremy. We're not in at the moment, but leave your name and number and we'll get back to you.*

It was her voice on the recording, bright, cheerful, and sounding quite unlike the person she actually was.

She pressed *96 followed by her four digit code, and waited to hear her messages.

There were never any.

Since her father had died six months ago, no one called them on their landline. Occasionally they talked about cancelling it, and then, because neither of them wanted to sort out the logistics, they let it drop.

But still she liked to check, dialling with the hope that perhaps there would be someone ringing with good news. Perhaps she'd won a lottery (not that she ever entered them), a distant relative had died and left her money in her estate, a long-lost admirer had resurfaced and wanted to tell her how much he missed and adored her — the moment of imagining was exquisite.

You have no messages.

And that was that.

The distraction was over.

She would have to wait a couple of hours before she called Jeremy to talk about what they would have for dinner.

Hannah worked in music licensing. She managed databases, making sure agreements were issued and invoices were paid. There was nothing glamorous about the job other than the very occasional free ticket to a gig that had failed to sell.

On the good days she didn't mind the work. There was a sense of completion when a round of payment notices were sent out, and satisfaction when the data was cleaned up. She also liked most of the people in the office; many had been performers or composers at some stage in their lives.

She'd played bass in a couple of cult bands that'd had record deals with indie labels. She still played at home and could occasionally be cajoled into a reunion gig for her own bands or for ones that she hadn't really been involved with but had made enough guest appearances with that it made sense for her to be part of their getting back together for one night only.

Any disappointment about the way her life had turned out was, for the most part, kept under control. She told herself she'd never really had the talent or dedication to make it. Besides, she'd always felt ambivalent about success. But there were days, like today, when the systems had crashed, and she spent hours looking at the clock while she surreptitiously searched the internet for a better place to rent.

And so she rang home earlier than usual, thinking that she might just allow herself two calls today.

On the third ring, it's answered. She must have dialled the wrong number.

Hello. The voice is croaky, cigarette rough and country broad.

Hannah apologises. She's made a mistake.

No you haven't. It's me. Jesus, love. It's your Dotty. Don't you know your own dog when you speak to her?

Hannah laughs. She hadn't known Jeremy was home. She certainly wouldn't have picked his voice. She laughs again, fine threads of nervousness pulling at the edge of her appreciation for his joke, as she asks him whether he is sick.

No more so than usual, love. Bored, yes. But I'm used to that. Hang here all day and sleep. Makes the time pass faster.

Occasionally bark at someone walking past the front gate. Dig up a bone if there's one lying around. Wait for you to get home.

Hannah gets up from her desk and goes to the compactus. Sliding open the doors, she slips into the filing shelves and tells Jeremy to cut it out.

The yawn on the other end of the phone sounds disturbingly like the dog's, followed by the jingle of the collar as she scratches herself. In the background Hannah can hear the next-door neighbour's Labrador barking.

There she goes again. Stupid bitch. Mad as a cut snake. See her down in the park and she looks right through you. Something not quite right in the head.

Hannah holds the phone away and looks at it.

You home soon? We going walking soon? You could leave the gate open, love. I'd just duck down there, have a quick sniff and scrounge, bring myself home. It's not like I don't know the way. Bit of a break in the day. Do me good.

'What happens if you were hit by a car?' Hannah sits on the ground and grins. She wouldn't have thought Jeremy had it in him. 'Or someone stole you and tried to turn you into one of those fighting dogs?'

I'm not going to walk in front of a car. It's not like I'm stupid. You know that. You've seen me roll over, play dead, spin, drop, heel.

The voice is silent for a moment. *And I'm past my prime. I might look rough and ready but you'd have to know there's not much fight left in me now. Strong, smart. But not a fighter.*

Hannah laughs nervously. 'You do growl at other dogs when you're on the lead.'

That's not fighting, but. You know what it's like, bit of nerves, bit of fear, can't do what I'd normally do. Why do you use that mouth collar, by the way? Never liked it. Didn't like that choke chain either. That was a bastard. Don't like any kind of lead come to think of it. Never had one before. Only when I came to you.

Outside the compactus, Wendy is sorting through files. Hannah looks up.

She and Jeremy have never had phone sex, and if they were going to start she certainly wouldn't engage in at it work, but there's something about this conversation that is uncomfortably close to a dirty phone call, the shame she feels at continuing akin to getting smutty in the office.

'So, what's for dinner tonight?' she asks, trying to bring it back to some normality.

There's another yawn at the end of the line. *Are you trying to be funny? Cup of dried biscuits for me. Something unbelievably good for you. The only hope I have is that you won't finish every mouthful and I'll get your scraps. Still, at least I get fed. I remember when I'd go days with nothing.*

Deciding to play along — after all, the systems are still down — Hannah asks if she (the dog), which must be he (Jeremy), is talking about the place she lived in before they adopted her from the rescue organisation. 'Where was it?' she asks. 'How did you end up lost?'

I don't know, love. Just didn't make it back to camp. We

were hunting pigs. I sniffed them out. We ran for miles. I got snagged in bushes. By the time I got out and came back, they'd all gone. And then I was in that cage. With that mad bastard of a dog. That was bad. Then someone took me and next thing I know, here I am.

Not entirely satisfied, Hannah stretches her legs out and leans back against the shelves. 'Did you like being a pig hunter? I mean, it must have been more fun than life now.'

Just different.

There's the sound of scratching, snuffling, and then a loud fart. Hannah snorts and is about to tell Jeremy enough is enough, if he's that good he's wasted in IT, he should be on the stage, when Wendy indicates that she needs to come in this row. Hannah raises a hand in apology and stands.

Two rows down, she slides back to the floor.

'Where were we?' she asks.

You expect me to remember?

'I do actually. You remember everything. We go to the park and pass a rotting bit of food, I drag you on, and you go back to exactly the same spot every morning for the next week.'

True.

There's a moment's silence, and the bark that follows it is loud enough for Hannah to remove the phone from her ear. 'Jesus, was that really necessary?'

Probably not. Just hate that little dog and need to let her know each time she comes past the gate. She snarls at me every time she sees me. Tried to bite me once too. You were saying?

'I was wanting to know if you liked your old life better than the one you have now?' Hannah is irritated.

The response is suitably cowering. *No, love. This is my home. You're not thinking of getting rid of me, are you? Sending me somewhere else?*

There were times when the idea had appealed, but Hannah didn't admit to that now.

'I just worry about you being happy. We leave you alone all day. You spend most of the time sleeping. It's like you're a prisoner. I feel responsible. I feel guilty all the time.' She is surprised as she utters the words. 'I'm in a rut, I suppose. I don't have the energy for you that I should have.'

There is a yawn on the other end of the phone.

'When I was younger I didn't think so much. I was too busy experiencing. Probably a bit like what it's like for a dog. I was so much more in the moment. But now I spend a lot of my days killing time. I have too much space in which to think and worry. I think I need to change my life. I really do.'

There is silence on the other end. It takes an instant before she realises the dog has hung up. She looks down at the receiver in her hand and feels a strange rush of vertigo. Slowly, she pulls herself up to standing, her body wedged between two walls of the compactus, files in front of her, files behind her.

Wendy looks in. 'You okay?'

Hannah nods.

WE ALL LIVED IN BONDI THEN

We all lived in Bondi then, in flats that were two up, two down. Each had a long, dark corridor, with a double bedroom and sunroom at the front, followed by the smaller bedroom, looking out onto a brick wall.

The bathrooms had chipped enamel baths and a mirrored cupboard wedged between two narrow windows. The hall ended at a lounge that opened onto a kitchen/dining room, wooden fretwork separating the two spaces.

Most of these apartments were carpeted in tired browns or greens; the slightly fancier ones had polished boards. We furnished them with op shop and street finds: sagging club lounges, glass-topped deco coffee tables, and wooden beds with rusted springs. Our art consisted of posters, our saucepans were aluminium with anodised lids in jade green and fire-engine red, and our crockery and cutlery was a jumble of hand-me-downs.

These were the days before we knew about Danish design, or copper-based pots, the days before we atomised into solidified couples, children, and mortgages, buying houses on the other side of Sydney where the streets were hot and empty, the arterial roads choked with traffic.

It was late summer when we had that party. I think it was for Henry's birthday, but I don't remember how old he was. Maybe twenty-three?

Henry and I lived downstairs, so we laid claim to the patch of cracked concrete outside our back door. We draped the Hills Hoist with tinsel and streamers, we borrowed chairs and trestle tables, and we filled the cement sinks in the laundry with ice from the service station. Jeanie picked up the pastizzis from the Maltese café in Surry Hills and Bryn took charge of the music.

I was making cocktails, blending liberal dashes of spirits with juice, ice, and fruit, the lino in the kitchen slippery with spilt daiquiri and mojito, as I offered glasses to everyone.

It was all in full swing when Jimmy arrived.

'Lucy and I are getting married,' Henry told him, putting his arm around me as he introduced us.

I rolled my eyes.

The night before we had fought, as we often did. He

was leaving on tour in two days, and he always became more insecure before he went. I didn't know that then — I wasn't particularly given to analysing our relationship — but in retrospect, I saw the pattern.

The argument began when I told him I wouldn't take him to the airport.

'But you can miss a shift,' he'd complained.

The truth was, I could. But I had reached the stage of withdrawing so much from his need that my habit was *not* to give, and then he sulked, until I relented, worn down by his bad temper.

After we had fought and made up, he had woken me. Drunks were coming home from the pub, their shouts loud on the street. He leant out the window, his long lean body white in the moonlight, and told them to *shut the fuck up* before closing the doors to the sunroom and sliding back into bed.

'We should get married,' he whispered.

I pretended to be asleep.

'Will you marry me?'

It was not the first time he had asked me, and each time I had either failed to answer or laughed the question off.

Now as he stood there with Jimmy, he declared that I was the love of his life before tossing back one of the cocktails I had made, taking another, and moving into the lounge room where he began to sway to the music.

Henry was a dancer. He was in a troupe that was

always on the verge of success. They were invited to fringe festivals here and overseas, they often received glowing reviews, but they were always broke.

When I first met him, he swung from the rafters in an attempt to impress me. Which he did. Rarely had I seen a body move with such grace.

Jimmy smiled at me. 'So. You're engaged? I wouldn't have pegged you for the type.'

I handed him a cocktail and stepped out from behind the table. His eyes had the empty blackness of night and his hair fell in loose glossy curls. He had a scar running down his left cheekbone, and long, fine hands that no doubt could unzip a dress as fast as a wink. He wore an op shop suit and an emerald green shot-silk shirt that hung, slightly rumpled over the top of his trousers — one button undone to reveal a smooth stomach.

'Why haven't I met you before?' I asked, drunk as a skunk and ready to flirt.

Together, we leant against the kitchen bench. I'd kicked my shoes off and I hoisted myself up to sit on the counter, my gaze level with his. Out of the corner of my eye, I could see Henry's reflection in the lounge-room mirror, his back moving slowly as he talked to Lou, the cocktail he was clutching slopping over the edge of the glass.

Jimmy's body was warm next to mine.

He'd only just joined the dance group, he told me. He'd been brought in when Martin was injured, to help out with the show for the festival.

He smiled, just slightly. 'You don't go on tour with your fiancé?'

I shook my head.

'Shame.'

And I raised my eyebrows.

'I'd heard about you, you know. From Henry,' he added moments later. 'And I saw you on that show. You're different to how I imagined.'

I'd played a junkie on a police series recently — four episodes, enough to get me occasionally recognised, and to bring in further auditions, always for the prostitute with a drug problem.

'Henry got lucky.' He paused here, dark eyes fixed on mine.

He was rolling a spliff, which he handed to me, the tips of those beautiful fingers touching my wrist for a moment. The sweet smell of grass, sugary cocktails, and underneath it all, the salt of the ocean breeze.

I drew back, holding the smoke in, grinning as I did so. 'You're pretty forward, you know.'

He had a slight gap between his front teeth.

'I guess so,' he said. 'I just saw you and liked you.'

He stood up then, his body no longer leaning against the bench, and I didn't want him to go.

Outside someone put on Prince, 'Sign of the Times', and I told him I was going to dance. 'Want to join me?'

His grin was slow. 'Sure.'

If I sound callous, it's because I was — or at least that's how my behaviour would be interpreted now that we're all in this different land, a land in which we understand the reason behind commitment. But then we were like moths, fluttering blindly towards whatever light flickered brightest.

I had been with Henry for three years, and for the last two, I had no longer been in love. He knew that and yet he chose to stay. I knew that; the knowledge that what we had was only temporary ran underneath our lives together, sure and steady as any commitment.

Sometimes he slept with other women, hoping to rouse my anger, I suppose. He didn't tell me, but the clues he left were so obvious, he might as well have confessed. I never rose to the bait. Nor was I ever unfaithful to him.

And yet, despite this lack of love on my part, a lot of the time we lived together in relative harmony, friends who enjoyed going out together, who sought out the company of the same people, who laughed at the same strange moments in life, and who could walk into a room and read it in the same way. Later I wondered at his decision to stay. Later I realised he probably hoped I was going to change. But I didn't think about it then. We were just young.

With the spliff in my hand, I danced, more alone than with Jimmy, but aware of where he was, the shot silk of that shirt slithering like a green snake, shimmering in the beautiful rich gold afternoon light. Outside, someone was hosing down the concrete, the laughter rising above the hiss of the water on the heat, and in the kitchen someone else had taken over the blender, ice whirring in a crush of pineapple and strawberry and mango. In the hallway I caught the occasional glimpse of Henry, leaning in close to Lou, pressing her against the wall, his back to me so that I couldn't see his face, whether he was angry or flirting with her. Not that I cared.

'Want to go for a swim?' Jimmy whispered in my ear, and I nodded, eyes closed as the song was put on again, the needle clicking into the wrong groove momentarily before slipping into the opening bars.

I loved the evenings in Bondi, the drift of the salt off the sea, the bruised gold of the ocean, the laziness of people strolling along the promenade, and the flicker of the streetlights as they came on, high above the beachfront.

'I want to always live here,' I told Jimmy.

Far off at the south end I could see the white walls of Icebergs, darkening. The north was still lit by the last rays of the sun, and in between the waves heaved, slow and sure, a swell that had risen with the full moon.

Last birthday, Henry had written a message for me along the wall that dropped down from the promenade to the sand. *Lucy — love you forever!*, scrawled in old house paint, large enough to read from one end of the beach or the other.

I could see it as I swam out into the sea with Jimmy,

my hair slick down my back, the cold of the ocean running like silver through my veins.

'Is that you?' he asked.

I nodded.

His hand around my back drew me close and I kissed him, salty mouth on salty mouth. Neither of us said we shouldn't be doing this.

'I wish I could take you home,' Jimmy said.

'You could,' I told him.

He shook his head, teeth white against the darkness of his tan, drops of water sparkling on his long lashes. 'I'm on a lounge-room floor until we leave for Adelaide. But when I get back,' he promised. 'When I get back, I'll have my own place and —' he smiled then. 'I can't believe this,' he splashed at the water with his palm. 'How did this happen?'

I laughed.

'I've always wanted to meet someone like you, and now I have.'

Back at the apartment, the party was over.

'He's in there,' Jeanie told me, pointing to our room.

She was sweeping up the last of the broken glasses, hired from the place on Bronte Road.

Only a few people remained, huddled outside together, talking and smoking joints. I could vaguely make out Mikey and Lila, and perhaps it was Lou, crying.

The music was still playing, but softly — a mixed tape that I'd once made for Henry. Sad songs.

I didn't want to go into our room. I hated our room. I hated the smell of him on our sheets, I hated his clothes hanging in our wardrobe and off the picture rails, I hated the poster he'd hung above our chest of drawers, I hated our underclothes mingled together.

'What happened?' I asked Jeanie.

She just looked at me and shook her head. 'Where'd you go?'

I told her I'd gone for a swim.

Henry was lying on our bed, eyes closed in the darkness.

Next to him was a packet of painkillers, the ones with codeine that we both liked taking when we'd been out all night on speed or cocaine or ecstasy. I picked up the box and shook it. There were plenty left.

As he turned to face me, I saw he'd been crying, the skin around his eyes puffy and pink. His breath smelt sour, and I flinched slightly, pulling away, but his grip on my hand was tight.

He didn't say anything. He just stared at me, harsh and hard, with a touch of the demon in his look, a slightly maniacal glare that he favoured when he wanted me to know that he was Slipping Over the Edge. Because Henry was a drama queen. He always had been.

And then he got up and went out to the little that remained of the party, pouring himself a straight rum in the kitchen and cranking up the music as he stepped out into the courtyard.

Standing at the back window, I watched him as he grabbed Lou and began to dance with her, pulling her close until she pushed him away and told him to fuck off.

Within the next ten minutes, everyone left, muttering goodbyes to each other as they walked up the side path, leaving us as hastily as they could.

We were alone now, and I packed my toothbrush and underpants, telling him I was going to stay at a friend's house, I didn't want to be with him, not when he was like this.

Holding my hand tight within his own, Henry cried and cried; he was sorry he'd kissed Lou, he was sorry about everything, he didn't want to lose me, he didn't want me to go.

I didn't understand. Maybe he didn't know about Jimmy, or maybe he was mucking with my head, or maybe we were both so drunk that nothing made any sense.

'Please stay,' he begged.

Exhausted now, I lay down on the crumpled sheets next to him, the smell of alcohol and cigarette smoke from the party mingled with the saltiness of my own skin.

'We'll make it better when I get back,' he promised, the softness of his hair warm against my side.

I didn't say anything. I just waited for him to fall asleep and then I lay there, all of me a-fizz with the thought of Jimmy.

* * *

Henry was gone for three weeks. He called me every Sunday, ringing from a payphone because in those days it was expensive to call interstate; in those days, we didn't send emails or texts; in those days, things were different.

The show was a success, he said, people loved it. They were sold-out every night. Even Nina Simone had come.

'There's talk about going to London next year. Maybe even France as well.'

And then he would tell me that he missed me, that he was looking forward to coming home.

I didn't dare ask him about Jimmy. I didn't dare mention his name. But each night before I went to sleep, I imagined him, drawing him just as he was, that gap-toothed grin, his hair like rumpled silk beneath my fingers, and those lips, salty and warm. When they came back, I would go, I told myself. I would pack my bags and move to another flat in Bondi, another home with someone I loved.

It was Henry who mentioned him, who asked me if I remembered that guy, Jimmy. 'He was at my party,' he said. 'He liked you.'

'Sure,' I replied, my voice even and calm.

'He's a fuckwit,' Henry said. 'We had to boot him out. Rejig the show around him. But it's better now.'

I didn't speak.

'Someone stole from Lisa. Lesley was sure it was him.

But it wasn't just that. He was arrogant. Couldn't take direction. No one liked him.'

I asked where he'd gone.

'Who knows.'

I could hear Henry lighting a cigarette, and then he muttered something to someone waiting near the phone box.

'Back to Melbourne, I guess.'

He told me he had to go. They were all going out dancing. He couldn't wait to see me. 'Just one more night,' he said. 'Love you.'

I stood in our lounge room, the phone in my hand, and I looked out the back window to the night sky, illuminated by all the windows around us, flats like ours, two up, two down, and then I hung up the phone.

I never saw Jimmy again. All I knew was that he was a dancer, good-looking, and he lived in Melbourne. Or maybe he didn't. Once when I was drunk, I asked Lisa if she knew what had happened to him. She was about to answer and then she became distracted, another friend had arrived, someone she hadn't seen for ages, and as they embraced and exclaimed and looked at each other in amazement, I just drifted off.

Henry lives in Leichhardt now. He has a son and a partner, and he teaches drama at a local high school. The few times I see him, pushing a pram or shopping, we ignore each other. I eventually left him for someone else and I know he hated me for a long time.

I live in Newtown, in a small semi, with a courtyard out the back. I haven't had an acting job in years, and most of my work is in events administration. When the nights are hot, our house baking from another long, humid day, Simon and I sometimes drive down to the beach. We sit on the grass, drinking beer and eating fish and chips, while the seagulls wheel above us, ghostly white in the salty mist.

'It's still there,' Simon always says, and he points it out to me, although I have already checked it.

Just one word left from Henry's graffiti.

Forever, scrawled in house paint along the wall.